THE PENNILESS LORDS

In want of a wealthy wife

Meet Daniel, Gabriel, Lucien and Francis.
Four lords: each down on his fortune and
each in need of a wife of means.

From such beginnings, can these marriages
of convenience turn into something
more treasured than money?

Don't miss this enthralling new quartet by
Sophia James

Read Daniel and Gabriel's stories in

Marriage Made in Money
Already available

Marriage Made in Shame
Out now

Author Note

Marriage Made in Shame is the second book in **The Penniless Lords** quartet, and Gabriel's story has been a delight to write.

I took his problem to the book club I have been in for twenty years, with twelve of my closest friends, and we had such a great time discussing just exactly how he might be cured.

He's a complex, enigmatic hero, who needed an interesting and unusual heroine for his happy-ever-after.

Lady Adelaide Ashfield is a wealthy bluestocking with her own particular demons and a desperate need to be loved.

Daniel (Book 1 *Marriage Made in Money*), Lucien (Book 3), and Francis (Book 4) are also part of the story—and so is Christine, Lucien's sister, who keeps popping her head in everywhere.

I hope you enjoy *Marriage Made in Shame*.

I love any feedback, and can be found on sophiajames.co.

MARRIAGE MADE IN SHAME

Sophia James

First published in Great Britain 2015
by Mills & Boon, an imprint of Harlequin (UK) Limited,
Large Print edition 2016
Harlequin (UK) Limited, Eton House, 18-24 Paradise Road,
Richmond, Surrey TW9 1SR

© 2015 Sophia James

ISBN: 978-0-263-26272-8

Harlequin (UK) Limited's policy is to use papers that are natural,
renewable and recyclable products and made from wood grown in
sustainable forests. The logging and manufacturing processes conform
to the legal environmental regulations of the country of origin.

Printed and bound in Great Britain
by CPI Antony Rowe, Chippenham, Wiltshire

Sophia James lives in Chelsea Bay, on Auckland, New Zealand's North Shore, with her husband, who is an artist. She has a degree in English and History from Auckland University and believes her love of writing was formed by reading Georgette Heyer in the holidays at her grandmother's house. Sophia enjoys getting feedback at sophiajames.co.

Visit the Author Profile page
at millsandboon.co.uk for more titles.

Chapter One

London—1812

The familiar sense of nothingness engulfed Gabriel Hughes, the fourth Earl of Wesley, taking all breath and warmth with it as he sat with a glass of fine brandy and a half-smoked cheroot.

Willing women dressed as sprites, nymphs and naiads lounged around him, the white of their scanty togas falling away from generous and naked breasts. A dozen other men had already chosen their succour for the night and had gone one by one to the chambers fanning out from the central courtyard. But here the lights were dimmed and the smoke from dying candles curled up towards the ceiling. The Temple of Aphrodite was a place of consenting lust and well-paid liaisons. It was also filled to the brim.

'I should very much like to show you my charms in bed, *monsieur*,' the beautiful blonde next to him whispered in a French accent over-laid with a heavy, east London twang. 'I have heard your name mentioned many times before and it is said that you have a great prowess in that department.'

Had... The word echoed in Gabriel's mind and reverberated as a shot would around a steel chamber. Downing the last of the brandy, he hoped strong alcohol might coax out feelings he had long since forgotten. Memory. How he hated it. His heartbeat quickened as he swallowed down disquiet, the hollow ache of expectation not something he wanted to feel.

'I am Athena, my lord.'

'The sister of Dionysus?'

She looked puzzled by his words as she flicked the straps from milky white shoulders and the warm bounty of her bosom nudged against his arm as she leant forward. 'I do not know this sister of Diana, my lord, but I can be yours tonight. I can pleasure you well if this be your favour.'

He hadn't expected her to know anything of the Greek gods, but still disappointment bloomed—a woman of beauty and little else. Her tongue ran around pouting lips, wetting them and urging re-sponse, dilated pupils alluding to some opiate, a whore without shame or limit and one whom life had probably disappointed. Feeling some sense of kinship, Gabriel smiled.

'You are generous, Athena, but I cannot take you up on your offer.'

Already the demons were arching, coming closer, and when her fingers darted out to cup his groin, he almost jumped. 'And why is that, *monsieur*? The Temple of Aphrodite is the place where dreams are realised.'

Or nightmares, he thought, the past rushing in through the ether.

Screams as the fire had taken hold; the sting-ing surprise of burning flesh and then darkness numbing pain. The last time he had felt whole.

Gabriel hated it when these flashbacks came, unbidden, terrifying. So sudden that he had no defence against them. Standing, he hoped that Athena did not see the tremble in his fingers as he replaced his empty glass on the low-slung table. Run, his body urged even as he walked slowly across the room, past the excesses of sex, passion and craving. He hated the way he could not quite ingest the cold night air once outside as the roiling nausea in his stomach quickened and rose.

He nearly bumped into the Honourable Frank Barnsley and another man as Gabriel strode out into the gardens and he looked away, the sweat on his upper lip building. He knew he had only a matter of minutes to hide all that would come next.

There were trees to his left, thick and green, and he made for them with as much decorum as he could manage. Then he was hidden, bending, no longer quite there. It was getting worse. He was falling apart by degrees, the smell of heavy perfumes, the full and naked flesh, the tug of sex and punch of lust. All equated with another time, another place. Intense guilt surfaced, panic on the edges. His heart thumped and fear surged, the sensation of falling so great he simply sat down and placed his arms around the solid trunk of a young sapling. A touchstone. The only stable thing in his moving dizzy world.

Leaning over to one side, he threw up once and then twice more, gulping in air and trying to understand.

His life. His shame.

Coming tonight to the Temple of Aphrodite and expecting a healing had been a monumental mistake. He needed to lie down in dark and quiet. Aloneness cloaked dread as tears began to well.

'I do not wish to marry anyone, Uncle.' Miss Adelaide Ashfield thought her voice sounded shrill, even to her own ears, and tried to moderate the tone. 'I am more than happy here at Northbridge and the largesse that is my inheritance can be evenly divided between your children, or their children when I die.'

Alec Ashfield, the fifth Viscount of Penbury, merely laughed. 'You are young, my dear, and that is no way to be talking. Besides, my offspring have as much as they are ever likely to need and if your father and mother were still in the land of the living, bless their poor departed souls, they would be castigating me for your belated entry into proper society.'

Adelaide shook her head. 'It was not your fault that Aunt Jean died the month before I was supposed to be presented in London for my first Season or that Aunt Eloise took ill the following summer just before the second.'

'But your insistence on an overly long mourning period was something I should have discouraged. You have reached the grand old age of three and twenty without ever having stepped a foot into civil society. You are, as such, beyond the age of a great match given that you no longer bear the full flush of youth. If we wait any longer, my love, you will be on the shelf. On the shelf and staying there. A spinster like your beloved great-aunts, watching in on the life of others for ever.'

'Jean and Eloise were happy, Uncle Alec. They enjoyed their independence.'

'They were bluestockings, my dear, without

any hope of a favoured union. One had only to look at them to understand that.'

For the first time in an hour Adelaide smiled. Perhaps her aunts had been overly plain, but their brains had been quick and their lives seldom dull.

'They travelled, Uncle, and they read. They knew things about the body and healing that no other physician did. Books gave them a world far removed from the drudge of responsibility that a married woman is encumbered by.'

'Drudges like children, like love, like laughter. You cannot know what seventy years in your own company might feel like and loneliness has no balm, I can tell you that right now.'

She looked away. Uncle Alec's wife, Josephine, had been an invalid for decades, secreted away in her chamber and stitching things for people who had long since lost the need for them.

'One Season is all I ask of you, Adelaide. One Season to help you understand everything you would be missing should you simply bury yourself here in the backwaters of rural Sherborne.'

Adelaide frowned. Now this was new. He would stipulate a limited time. 'You would not harry me into a further Season if this one is a failure?'

Alec shook his head. 'If you have no one offering for you, no one of your choice, that is, then I will feel as if my duty to your parents is done and you can come home. Even if you agree to stay half of the Season I would be happy.'

'From April till June. Only that?'

'Early April to late June.' There was a tone of steel in her uncle's voice.

'Very well. Three months. Twelve weeks. Eighty-four days.'

Alec laughed. 'And not one less. You have to promise me.'

Walking to the window, Adelaide looked out over the lands of Northbridge. She did not want to leave this place. She didn't want to be out in the glare of a society she had little interest in. She wanted to stay in her gardens and her clinic, helping those about Northbridge with the many and varied complaints of the body. Her world, ordered and understood; the tinctures and ointments, the drying herbs and forest roots. Safe.

'As I would need gowns and a place to live

and a chaperon, it seems like a lot of bother for nothing.'

'I have thought of all of these things and a relative of mine, Lady Imelda Harcourt, will accompany you.' As she went to interrupt Alec stopped her. 'I realise she is a little dour and sometimes more than trying, but she is also a respectable widow with undeniably good contacts amongst the *ton*. I, too, will endeavour to visit London as much as I am able whilst you are there. Bertram will want to have some hand in it as well, as he has assured me his gambling habits are now well under control.'

Her heart sank further. Not only Lady Harcourt but her cousin, too? What else could go wrong?

However, Uncle Alec was not quite finished. 'I wasn't going to mention this, but now seems like the perfect time to bring it up. Mr Richard Williams from Bishop's Grove has approached me with the hopes that he might be an escort whom you would look favourably upon during your time in town. A further arrow to our bow, so to speak, for we do not want you to be bereft of suitors. One day I am sure you will be thankful for such prudence. Here you are well known, Adelaide, but in London it can be difficult to meet others and a first impression has importance.'

Adelaide was simply struck dumb. She was being saddled with three people who would hardly be good company and her uncle expected her to thank him? It was all she could do to stay in the room and hear him out.

'Men will know you have a fortune and there are some out there who could be unscrupulous in their promises. Great wealth comes with its own problems, my dear, and you will need to be most careful in your judgement. Pick a suitor who is strong in his own right, a man whose fortune might equal your own. A good man. A solid man. A man of wealth and sense. Stay well away from those who only require a rich wife to allow them back into the gambling halls, or ones whose family estates have been falling around their feet for years.'

'I am certain I shall know exactly whom to stay away from, Uncle.' Privately she hoped that every single male of the *ton* would want to keep their distance from her and after this she would never have to be beleaguered by such ridiculous frippery again.

The doctor's rooms were in a discreet and well-heeled part of Wigmore Street and Gabriel had had it on good authority from the books he had acquired over the past months that Dr Maxwell Harding was the foremost expert on illnesses pertaining to problems in men of a more personal nature.

He almost had not come, but the desperation and despondency caused by his condition had led him to arrive for the earliest appointment at noon.

No other people graced the waiting area and the man behind a wide desk gave the impression of disinterest. For that at least Gabriel was glad. He did toy with the thought of simply giving a false name and was about to when the door behind him opened and an older man walked out.

'It is Lord Wesley, is it not? I am Dr Maxwell Harding. I have heard your name about town, of course, but have not had the pleasure of meeting you. In my line of work you are the one many of my patients would aspire to emulate, if you take my meaning, so this is indeed a surprise.' His handshake was clammy and he brought a hand-kerchief from his pocket afterwards to wipe his brow in a nervous gesture. 'Please, follow me.'

For Gabriel the whole world had just turned at an alarming rate. He did not wish for this doctor to know his name or his reputation. He certainly did not want to be told of a plethora of patients with their own sexual illnesses and hardships who all earmarked him as some sort of a solu-tion.

He suddenly felt almost as sick as he had a week ago outside the Temple of Aphrodite, but as the door behind him closed he took hold of himself. Harding was a doctor, for God's sake, pledged under the Hippocratic Oath to the wel-fare of each of his patients. It would be fine. The doctor had walked across to a cupboard now and was taking a decanter and two glasses from a shelf and filling them to the brim.

'I know why you are here, my lord,' Harding finally stated as he placed one in Gabriel's hands.

'You do?' With trepidation he took a deep swallow of the surprisingly good brandy and waited. Was it marked on his face somehow, his difficulty, or in the worry of his eyes? Was there some sort of a shared stance or particular gait in those who came through this door for help? Hopelessness, perhaps, or fear?

'You are here about the Honourable Frank Barnsley, aren't you? He said you had looked at him strangely when he met you the other day. As if you knew. He implied that you might come and talk with me. He said his father was a good friend of yours.'

'Barnsley?' Gabriel could not understand exactly where this conversation was going though he vowed to himself that after he finished the drink he would leave. This was neither the time nor the place to be baring his soul and the doctor was sweating alarmingly.

'His predilection for...men,' Harding went on. 'He said you had seen him and Andrew Carrington embracing one another in the garden at some well-heeled brothel and wondered if you might begin making enquiries…'

Anger had Gabriel placing his glass carefully down upon a nearby table. Harding was not only a gossip, but a medic with no sense of confidentiality or professionalism. Before the outburst he had had no inkling of the sexual persuasions of either man and it was none of his business anyway. He could also just imagine the hushed tones of Harding describing Gabriel's own problems to all and sundry should he have decided to trust in the doctor's honour. He was damned thankful that he had not.

He'd buy Barnsley and Carrington a drink when he saw them next in his club as a silent measure of gratitude. But for now he had one final job to do.

'Mr Frank Barnsley is a decent and honourable man. If I hear you mention any of this, to anyone at all, ever again, I will be back and I promise that afterwards no one will hear your voice again. Do I make myself clear?'

A short and frantic nod was apparent and at that Gabriel simply opened the door and walked out of the building, into the sunshine and the breeze, a feeling of escaping the gallows surging over him, one part pure relief, though the other echoed despair.

He could never tell anybody. Ever. He would have to deal with his problem alone and in privacy. He would either get better or he would not and the thought of years and years of sadness rushed in upon him with an awful truth.

His reality. His punishment. His retribution.

But today had been like a reprieve, too, a genuine and awkward evasion of what might have come to pass. He was known across the *ton* for his expertise with the opposite sex and if the scale of his prowess had grown with the mounting rumour he had not stopped that, either, his downfall sharpened on lies.

This is what he had come to, here and now, walking along the road to his carriage parked a good two hundred yards from the doctor's rooms to secure privacy and wishing things could be different; he could be different, his life, his secrets, his sense of honour and morality and grace.

Once he had believed in all the glorious ideals the British Service had shoved down his throat. Integrity. Loyalty. Virtue. Principle. But no more. That dream had long gone in the face of the truth.

He was alone in everything he did, clinging to the edge of life like a moth might to a flame and being burned to a cinder. There was nowhere else, or no one else. This was it.

He had always been alone and he always would be.

Chapter Two

Two weeks in the London Season had already seemed like a month and this was the fourth ball Adelaide had been to in as many nights. The same grandeur, the same people, the same boring chatter concerned only with marriage prospects, one's appearance and the size of a suitor's purse.

She was tired of it, though tonight the crowd was thicker and those attending did not all have the rarefied look of the *ton.* A less lofty gathering, she decided, and hence more interesting. Lady Harcourt beside her did not look pleased.

'Lord and Lady Bradford are rumoured to be enamoured by the changing tides of fortune and one can see that in some of the guests present—a lot of wealth but no true class. Perhaps we should not have come at all, Penbury?'

Her uncle only laughed and finished his drink. 'Adelaide isn't a green girl, Imelda, and I am certain she can discern whom to speak with and whom to avoid. In truth, even those with genuine titles seem to be rougher these days, less worried by the way a fortune is made or lost.' His eyes fixed on a group of men in the corner.

At that very moment the tallest of them raised his glass and said something that made the others laugh. Adelaide noticed he wore a thick band of silver around one of his fingers and that the cuff on his shirt was intricately embroidered in bronze thread. He was everything she had never liked in a man, a fop and a dandy, handsome to the point of beautiful and knowing it. Nearly every woman in the salon looked his way.

From her place to one side of a wide plastered pillar she watched him, too. Out of a pure and misplaced appreciation, she supposed, the length of his hair as extraordinary as every other feature upon him.

'The Earl of Wesley is the most handsome man in the King's court, would you not say, Miss Ashfield?' Miss Lucy Carrigan's voice rose above the chatter, breathless and adoring. 'It is understood that his London town house has mirrors on every wall so that he might look at himself from all possible angles.'

'And he would boast of this?' The frown that never left the forehead of Lucy Carrigan deepened.

'Well, if you were that beautiful, Miss Ashfield, should you not wish to look upon your form, too?'

Adelaide could only laugh at such a thought. My goodness, the girl was serious. She struggled to school in her mirth and find kindness.

'Perhaps it would be so.'

'My cousin Matilda said Lord Wesley kissed her once when she was much younger and she has never forgotten the feelings his expertise engendered. Indeed, she is long married and yet she still brings up the subject every few months.'

'And her husband is happy to hear this?'

'Oh, Norman can hardly object. It was Lord Wesley himself who introduced them to each other and steered them on to the pathway of Holy Matrimony.'

'Which he believes in?'

'Pardon?'

'The earl? Is he married?'

Peals of laughter were the only answer. 'Oh, dear me, no. A man like that is hardly going to be tied down to one female, is he, though word has it he did come close.'

'Close?'

'To Mrs Henrietta Clements. Some dreadful accident took her life a few months back, but the whole thing was hushed up quickly because she had left her wedded husband for Wesley. A scandal it was and the main topic of conversation for weeks after.'

Normally Adelaide stayed clear of such gossip, but fourteen days of society living had broken down her scruples somewhat and Lucy Carrigan for all her small talk was proving most informative.

'And so the earl was heartbroken?'

'Ahhh, quite the opposite. For a while nobody saw him at all, but then he began to spend far more time in the vicinity of fast women with questionable morals.'

'You speak of London's brothels?' Adelaide could not quite work out what she meant.

The other reddened considerably and dropped her voice. 'No lady of any repute should ever admit to knowing about such things, Miss Ashfield, even amongst friends.' Lucy Carrigan's eyes again perused the figure of the one they spoke about and Adelaide regarded him, too.

The Earl of Wesley was tall and broad with it, the foppish clothes out of character with his build. But the arrogance was not to be mistaken and nor was the intricately tied cravat that stood up under his chin and echoed the style of the day. The Mathematical, she had heard it called, with its three demanding and precise creases, one horizontal and two diagonal.

He stood with his back to the wall. Even as others came to join the group he was within, he still made certain that he faced any newcomer. And he watched. Everyone. Even her. She looked quickly away as bleached golden eyes fell by chance upon her face.

Lady Harcourt beside her was fussing about the heat in the room and the noise of the band.

Tired of listening to her constant stream of complaints, Adelaide signalled to her chaperon that she wished to use the ladies' retiring room and quietly moved away, glad when Imelda did not insist on accompanying her.

A moment later a small bench to one side of the salon caught her attention, a row of flowering plants placed before it allowing a temporary shelter. Glancing around to see that no one observed her, she pushed the greenery aside and slipped through, sitting down to stretch her legs. A row of windows before her overlooked a garden.

She had escaped, if momentarily, from the inane and preposterous world of being presented to society and she planned to enjoy every fleeting second of it.

'Ten more weeks,' she enunciated with feeling. 'Ten more damned weeks.'

A slight noise to one side had her turning and with shock she registered a man standing there. Not just any man, either, but the foppish and conceited Earl of Wesley.

Without being surrounded by admirers and sy-

cophants he looked more menacing and dangerous. Almost a different person from the one she
had been watching a few moments earlier if she
were honest. The pale gold of his eyes was startling as he looked towards her.

'Ten more damned weeks, until…what?'

A dimple in his right cheek caught the light of
a small flickering lamp a few feet away, sending
shadows across the face of an angel. A hardened
angel, she amended, for there was something in
his expression that spoke of distance and darkness.

'Until I can return home, my lord. Until this
dreadful society Season of mine is at last over.'
The honesty of her response surprised her. She
usually found strangers hard to talk to. Especially men who held all of the *ton* in thrall as
this one did.

'You do not enjoy the glamour and intrigue of
high courtly living, Miss…?'

'Miss Adelaide Ashfield from Northbridge
Manor.' When question crossed into his eyes she
continued. 'It is in Sherborne, my lord, in Dorset. I am the niece of the Viscount of Penbury.'

'Ahhh.' The one dimple deepened. 'You are rich, then, and well connected?'

'Excuse me?' She could not believe he would mention such a thing. Was that not just the very height of rudeness?

'My guess is that you are a great heiress who has come to the city on the lookout for a husband?'

'No.' The word came harshly and with little hidden.

He turned. Up close he was even more beautiful than he was from afar. If she could have conjured up a man from imagination personifying masculine grace and strength, it would have been him. The thought made her smile.

'You find society and its pursuit for sterling marriages amusing?' A bleak humour seemed to materialise on his face.

'I do not, sir. I find it degrading and most humiliating. The only true virtue in my list of attributes is wealth, you see, and as such I am… an easy target for those with dubious financial backgrounds.'

The returned laughter did not seem false. 'Such

a description of desperation might include half the lords of the *ton* then, Miss Ashfield. Myself included.'

'You are…penniless?' She could not believe he would be so candid.'

'Not quite, but heading that way.'

'Then I am sorry for it.'

The mirth disappeared completely. 'Do not be so. There is a freedom in such a state that is beguiling.'

Again Adelaide was perplexed. His words were not those of a vacuous and dandified lord. Indeed, this was the very first conversation that she had actually enjoyed since leaving Dorset.

He glanced around. 'Where is your chaperon, Miss Ashfield? I could hardly think she would be pleased to see you alone in my company.'

'Oh, Lady Harcourt is back amongst the crowd, complaining of the crush and the noise. I am supposed to be in the retiring room, you see, but I slipped off here instead.'

'A decision you might regret.'

'In what way, my lord?'

Now only ice filled the gold of his eyes. 'A reputation is easily lost amongst the doyens of the *ton*, no matter how little you do to deserve it.'

'I don't understand.'

He smiled. 'Stay close to your chaperon, Miss Ashfield, or one day you surely will.'

With that he was gone, a slight bow and then gone, only the vague scent of sandalwood remaining.

Adelaide breathed out deeply and pushed back the shrubbery, aware that others were now moving in her direction. Suddenly the room seemed larger and more forbidding than it had done before, an undercurrent of something she could not fathom, a quiet whisper of warning.

She had seen these weeks in the *ton* as both a game and a trial, but perhaps it was not quite either. To be roped into marriage on a mistake would be disastrous and life changing. Without pause she hurried back to Lady Harcourt.

She should not have been alone, Gabriel thought, watching as the unusual Miss Adelaide Ashfield rushed past him and back towards safety. She was so far from the usual run of those new to society he had barely believed she was one. Older for a start and much more…beguiling. Yes, that was the word. She did not seem to harbour the cunning and duplicity of almost every other débutante he had met. She was tall, too, her head rising to his chin, and at six foot four that was something that seldom happened. She was not blonde, either, her hair a mix of sable and dark chestnut and her eyes the colour of a winter stream running over limestone. Deep clear blue with shadows of hurt. He doubted the spectacles she wore were for any reason other than a way of making her appear more studious, less attractive. He could not remember seeing another woman ever wear spectacles to a ball. A further oddness that was intriguing.

Men who came for the Season with the hope of finding a docile and curvy blonde would not be interested in Miss Adelaide Ashfield from Sherborne.

'God,' he swore, but his eyes still followed her, pushing past other patrons, barely pausing.

He had frightened her. A good thing that. If one's reason for being in London for the Season was truly not marriage then she should be glued to the side of the harridan she had finally reached. Another man came to join her and Gabriel recognised him as the hapless Bertram Ashfield, no doubt newly come from the card rooms on one end of the salon. He looked defeated and luckless.

A taller man had also joined the party, his sallow face wreathed in smiles. He was talking to Miss Ashfield in the way of one whose words portrayed more than just the pure sounds. A suitor. Observing the way she leaned away from him, Gabriel gained the impression that any tender thoughts were not returned.

Perhaps she did not lie. Perhaps indeed she was here under duress. The scene became even more interesting when Frederick Lovelace, the Earl of Berrick, joined the small group in the company of the Viscount of Penbury himself. The baby-faced earl had the same look of hope in his expression as the other taller man had.

Gabriel smiled. Could Miss Ashfield be a siren perhaps with the penchant to attract men despite her wishing not to?

Look at her damned effect on him!

He rarely spoke with the new débutantes of the Season and certainly never for so long. Even now he wished he might find her again somewhere isolated so that they could converse further, the low and calm voice that did not hold back feelings placating somehow and sensible.

When the music began to play Gabriel knew it was a waltz and he watched as Berrick took Miss Ashfield's arm and led her on to the floor. All débutantes needed permission to dance the waltz and he wondered which of Almack's patronesses had allowed it.

The trouble was she did not seem to know the steps, tripping over her feet more times than he thought possible. Berrick held her closer and tighter so that she might follow him with a greater ease.

Hell. Why did the chaperon not intervene? Or the uncle? Did not others see how very inappropriate such closeness was? He glanced around, but no face was turned towards the couple in censure.

Perhaps Frederick Lovelace was further down

the pathway of his courtship than Miss Ashfield had let on? With a curse Gabriel turned for the door. An early night would do him good for once. If only he could sleep.

Adelaide saw Lord Wesley leave the room, the sure steps of his exit and the quiet observation of others. For one long and ridiculous moment she had imagined that he still watched her and that he might ask her to dance.

Instead the Earl of Berrick held her to the steps, his arms too tight and his body too close. The waltz must soon be finished, surely, and then pleading a headache she could leave, too. She was at that moment glad of such an elderly chaperon and one who would be more than happy for an early night.

Her uncle might not be so pleased, of course, but even he had begun to flag beneath the ludicrous constant social graces and late-night soirées of the *ton*. Bertie would stay, no doubt, locked into the card rooms in the hope of a win that never seemed to materialise.

'I should like to call upon you on the morrow if I may, Miss Ashfield.'

He looked as serious as she had ever seen another look. Would he be showing his hand as a suitor? Pray God, she hoped not, but when he squeezed her fingers and looked intently at her she knew that such a wish was false.

'You are a sensible girl, well endowed with a brain and the ability to use it.'

She smiled, hating her pasted-on joviality with an ache. She could never before remember playing people so false than here in London.

'My mother, the countess, would like you.'

The music stopped just as she thought she might burst into laughter and Lord Berrick could do nothing but escort her back to her chaperon.

For once the frowns of Lady Harcourt were reassuring and Adelaide took her hand.

'You are tired, Aunt. Perhaps we might leave?'

The older lady failed to hide the relief that flooded into her eyes as she leant upon her charge and they threaded through the crowded room to the exit.

Gabriel dreamed that night of colourful dresses and tuneful waltzes, and of a woman in his arms on the dance floor smelling of lemon and hope. Her dark hair was loose and her eyes mirrored the hue of the flowers the greenery around them was bedecked with.

But something was wrong. The ease of the dream turned into worry. He must not kiss her. She would know otherwise. He needed to find some distance from the softness of her touch, a way of leaving without causing question. But she was stuck to him like a spider's web, clinging and cold, and the only way to be rid of her was to push her down and down until she lay still beneath the marbled font of the destroyed wooden chapel, the smell of sulphur on the glowing fabric of her gown and her feet bare.

Henrietta Clements morphed from Adelaide Ashfield, the blonde of her hair pinked with blood.

He tried to shout, but no words came, tried to run, too, but his feet could not move and the burning ache on his upper right thigh pulled him from sleep into the cold and grey light of dawn.

He could barely breathe, his whole body stiffened in fright and the anger that hung quiet in the daytime now full blooded and red.

Henrietta had come to him out of fear, he knew that. Her husband was purportedly involved in helping to fund Napoleon's push into Europe and Gabriel had been tailing Randolph Clements for a month or so in an effort to find out more. The Service had had word of the man's close connections with others in London who held radical views and they wanted to see just whom he associated with.

A simple target. An easy mark. But the small notice he had allowed Henrietta Clements had changed into something else, something he should have recognised as dangerous from the very start.

He laughed, but the sound held no humour whatsoever. Since the fire Randolph Clements had gone to ground, hiding in the wilds of the northern borders, he supposed, or perhaps he had taken ship to France. It didn't matter much any more. If Clements wanted to exact revenge for the death of his wife, Gabriel would have almost welcomed it, an ending to the sorry saga that his life had now become.

The fire at Ravenshill had ruined him, completely, any intimacy and want for feminine company crouched now amongst pain and fury and sacrifice.

He'd broken hearts and promises for years whilst cutting a swathe through the capricious wants of unhappily married wives. Information to protect a country at war could be gathered in more ways than one might imagine and he done his patriotic duty without complaint.

The rumours that circled around about him had helped as he gathered intelligence whilst a sated paramour lay asleep. It was easy to sift his way through the contents of a husband's desk or safe or sabretache without prying eyes, and the danger of stepping into the lair of the enemy had been a great part of the enjoyment.

Until Henrietta Clements.

As he perceived his hand stroking the damaged skin on his right thigh he stopped and touched the silver-and-gold ring he had bought three months ago from the jewellers, Rundell and Bridges, in Ludgate Hill.

'The symbol engraved upon the circle is Christian, my lord, and of course the word engraved is Latin. *Fortuna*. Lady luck, and who cannot do with a piece of that.'

The salesman was an earnest young man Gabriel had not seen in the shop before and seemed to have a bent for explaining the spiritual. 'Luck is, of course, received from the faith a believer entrusts in it, for a talisman is only strong when there is that sense of conviction. We have other clients who swear by the advantages they have received. The safe birth of a babe. The curing of a badly broken arm. A cough that is finally cured after months of sleepless nights.'

The ability to make love again?

Did he believe? Gabriel thought. Could he afford not to? Once he would have laughed at such nonsense, but for now he was catching at rainbows and hope with all the fervour of the newly converted. He had paid a fortune for the questionable assistance and had worn it ever since. He wondered momentarily if he should not just snatch the trinket from his finger and throw it into the Thames, for twelve weeks with no sign at all of any inherent powers was probably a fairly conclusive sign of its lack of potency.

Yet hope held him to the wearing of it, even though his own condition had not changed one whit for the better.

It was a week later, despite all his attempts at desiring otherwise, that Gabriel Hughes finally accepted the fact that he was impotent.

He looked down at his flagging member in the darkened room off Grey Street and thought that this was where life had brought him. An ironic twist. An unwanted mockery of fate.

The woman in the bed was beautiful, bountiful and sweet—a country girl with the combination of dewy sensibleness and a sultry sensuality burning to be ignited. She sat there watching him, a clean and embroidered chemise the only thing covering her, a quiet smile on unpainted lips.

'I thought my first customer might be old and ugly, sir. I had wondered if I should even be able to do what my aunt has bidden me to, but I can see that this job is likely to be a lot less diffi- cult than my old one. I worked in a weaving mill, you see, but it closed down. It was me and a hundred other girls and the light hurt my eyes and we were never allowed to just stop. Not like this, sir. Never like this. Never on our backs in the warmth and with a glass of good wine for the drinking.'

'You are a virgin, then?' His heart sank at all such a state would imply.

She shook her head. 'Mary said I was to say I was 'cos the coinage is better that way, but I go to church on Sundays, sir, and could not abide by the lie.'

Gabriel was glad for this fact at least. The first time should be special for every woman. He be- lieved that absolutely.

'My Jack went and died on me before we were married. He got sick one day and was taken the next. It was just lucky that I did not catch the worst of it though I was ill for a good many weeks after.'

The barrage of information ran into the room

with an ease that held him still and listening. For the first time in a long while Gabriel did not wish to be away from the company of a half-naked woman with such desperation. Even the roiling nausea seemed to settle with her words, the information comforting somehow.

'Mam said I should come to London to her sister, who was doing more than well.' She shook her brown curls and laughed. 'I don't think she realises exactly what it is Aunt Mary is up to, but, with little other in the way of paying work back home, I agreed to come in and try it. We haven't yet though, have we?' And, with colourful language, she went on to say just what it was they hadn't yet done.

Gabriel turned towards the window. The phrases she used were coarse, but the talk was relaxing him. Perhaps such candour was what kept the blood from his ears and his breath even. Small steps in the right direction. Tiny increments back to a healing. If he could only stop thinking and do the deed once...

Reality brought his attention to the problem before him as he looked down. Flaccid. Unmoving. The scar tissue on his right thigh and groin in the light from the window was brutal and he pulled his breeches up.

But she was off the bed in a flash, one warm hand clutching his arm. 'Can you stay for a while, sir? Only a little while so that...' She stopped as though trying to formulate what she wanted to say next.

'So your aunt will think you at least earned your keep?'

'Exactly that, sir, and it is nice here talking with you. You smell good, too.'

He laughed at this and removed her hand. Sitting here was not the agony he had imagined after the fiasco in the Temple of Aphrodite and he gestured to her to pour more wine, which she did, handing it to him with a smile. His beaker was chipped on one side so he turned it around.

'Jack used to say we would be married with a dozen children before we knew it and look what happened to him. Life is like a game of chess, I'd be thinking. One moment you are winning everything and the next you are wiped off the board.'

'You play chess?'

'I do, sir. My father taught me when I were little. He was a mill worker, too, you understand, but a gent once taught him the rudiments of the game in a tavern out of Styal in Cheshire and he never forgot it. I have my board and pieces with me. We could play if you like? To waste a bit of time?'

The wine was cheap, but the room was warm and as the girl brought her robe off of a hook and wrapped it around herself, Gabriel breathed out.

Little steps, he reiterated to himself. Little tiny steps. And this was the first.

An hour later after a close game Gabriel extracted a golden guinea from his pocket and gave it to her. 'For your service, Sarah, and for your kindness.'

Bringing the coin between perfectly white teeth, she bit down upon it. Still young enough not to have lost them, still innocent enough to imagine that gold might be a cure for the dissolution of morality. A trade-off that at this point in her life still came down on the black side of credit. *God*, he muttered to himself as he grabbed his jacket.

Henrietta Clements had been the same once. Hopeful and blindly trusting.

He brought out his card from a pocket and laid it down on the lumpy straw mattress. 'Can you read?'

She shook her head.

'If you ever want to escape this place, find someone who can, then, and send word to me for help. I could find you more…respectable work.'

She was off of the bed in a moment, the scent of her skin pungent and sharp as she threaded her arms about his neck.

'If you lay down, I'd do all the work, sir. Like a gift to you seeing as you have been so nice and everything.'

Full lips closed over his and Gabriel could feel an earnest innocence. The pain of memory lanced over manners as he pushed her back.

'No.' A harsher sound than he meant, with things less hidden.

'You won't be calling again?' Sarah made no

attempt at hiding her disappointment. 'Not even for another game of chess?'

'I'm afraid I won't.' The words were stretched and quick, but as manners laced through reason he added others. 'But thank you. For everything.'

Chapter Three

The stone was cold, rubbed smooth with the echoes of time. He had tried to reach her, through the tapestries of Christ under thorns, but the choking smoke had stopped him, the only sound in his ears the one of a ghastly silence.

His dagger was in his fist, wrapped around anger, the Holy Water knocked from its place on the pulpit and falling on to marble pocked with time. The spectre of death had him, even as he reached for Henrietta, the trickle of red running down his fingers and her eyes lifeless.

Gabriel woke with the beat of his heart loud in his ears and his hands gripping the sheets beneath him.

The same bloody dream, never in time, never

quick enough to save her. He cursed into fingers cradled across his mouth, hard harsh words with more than a trace of bitterness within as his eyes went to the timepiece on the mantel.

Six o'clock. An hour's sleep at least. Better than some nights, worse than others. Already the first birds were calling and the working city moved into action. The street vendors with their words and their incantations. 'Milk maids below.' 'Four for sixpence, mackerel.' The heavier sound of a passing carriage drowned them out.

Unexpectedly the image of the water-blue eyes of Miss Adelaide Ashfield came to mind, searing through manners and propriety on the seat at the edge of the Bradfords' ballroom as she cursed about her ten more weeks.

Where did she reside in London? he wondered. With her uncle in his town house on Grosvenor Square or in the home of Lady Harcourt? Did she frequent many of the *ton*'s soirées or was she choosy in her outings?

Swearing under his breath, he rose. He had no business to be thinking of her; she would be well counselled to stay away from him and as soon as he had caught those who were helping Clements in his quest for Napoleon's ascendency he, too, would be gone.

The society mamas were more circumspect with him now, the failing family fortune common knowledge and the burned-out shell of the Wesley seat of Ravenshill Manor unattended. His father had squandered most of what had been left to them after his grandfather's poor management, and Gabriel had been trying to consolidate the Wesley assets ever since. The bankers no longer courted him, neither did the businessmen wanting the backing of old family money to allow them an easy access to ideas. It would only be a matter of time before society turned its back altogether.

But he'd liked talking with Adelaide Ashfield from Dorset. This truth came from nowhere and he smiled. God, the unusual and prickly débutante was stealing his thoughts and he did not even want to stop and wonder why.

She reminded him of a time in his life when things had been easier, he supposed, when conflict could be settled with the use of his fists and when he had gone to bed at midnight and slept until well past the dawn.

What would happen after the allotted ten weeks? Would her uncle allow her to simply slip back into the country with her fortune intact, unmarried and free?

His eyes rested upon the gold locket draped on the edge of an armoire to one side of the window.

The bauble had been Henrietta's. She had left it here the last time she had come to see him and he had kept it after her death. For safekeeping or a warning—the reminder of love in lost places and frozen seconds? For the memory of why a close relationship would never again be something that he might consider? He had tried to remember how the fire in the chapel had begun, but every time he did so there was a sense of something missing.

For a while he imagined it might have been he who had started it, but subsequently he had the impression of other hands busy with that very purpose. Hers? Her husband's? The men they associated with? The only thing Gabriel was certain of was the hurt and the stab of betrayal that had never left him.

But perhaps he and Miss Adelaide Ashfield were more alike than he thought? Perhaps she had been hurt, too, by someone, by falsity, by promise. It was not often, after all, that a young and beautiful girl held such an aversion to marriage and stated it so absolutely.

He would like to meet her again just to understand what it was that she wanted. The Harveys were holding a ball this very evening and perhaps the Penbury party had the intention of going? He had heard that Randolph Clements's cousin George Friar might be in attendance and wanted to get a measure of the man. Wealthy in his own right, the American had been staying with the Clements for a good while now, but some said he was a man who held his own concealments and darkness.

The inlaid gold on his ring glinted in the light and Gabriel frowned as he recited the Anglican prayer of resurrection beneath his breath. Turning the circle of gold and silver against his skin, he positioned it so that the inlaid cross faced upwards.

Fortuna.

He suddenly felt that he had lost the hope of such a thing a very long time ago.

Arriving at the Harveys' ball later than he meant to, the first person Gabriel met was his friend Daniel Wylde, the Earl of Montcliffe, with Lucien Howard, the Earl of Ross, at his side.

'I am only down from Montcliffe for a few days, Gabe, trying to complete a deal on the progeny of a particularly fine pair of greys I own.'

Gabriel's interest was piqued. 'The Arabian beauties that were standing at Tattersall's a year or so back? The ones that caused a stir before they were pulled from auction.'

'The very same. Perhaps you might be interested in a foal for the Ravenshill stables?' Lucien Howard's voice was threaded with an undercurrent of question.

'My means are about as shaky as your own are

rumoured to be, Luce. I doubt I could afford to feed another horse, let alone buy one.'

Daniel Wylde laughed heartily before any more could be said. 'Find a wife, then, who is both beautiful and rich. That's your answer.'

'Like you did?'

'Well, in all truth, she found me...'

The small and round Miss Greene and her younger sister chose that moment to walk past and gaze in Gabriel's direction. He had stood up with her in a dance earlier in the Season as a favour to their bountifully blessed aunt and the girls had seemed to search him out at each ensuing function.

A plethora of other ladies milled around behind them, each one seemingly younger than the next. And then to one corner he noticed Miss Adelaide Ashfield. Tonight she was adorned in gold silk, the rich shade making her hair look darker and her skin lighter.

She was laughing at something the girl beside her had said though at that very moment she looked up and caught Gabriel's glance. From this distance he could see something in her eyes that drew out much more in his expression than he wanted to show. With shock he broke the contact, his heart hammering.

Not sexual, but an emotion far more risky. He almost swore, but a footman chose that exact moment to pass by with an assortment of drinks on a silver tray.

The liquor slid across panic and soothed it. He saw the question that passed between Montcliffe and Ross, but he turned away, the card room as good a place as any to drown his sorrows.

'If you will excuse me, I might try my hand at a game of whist.'

'But a waltz is about to begin, Gabe, and the girl in gold in that corner looks as though she would welcome a dance.'

He left saying nothing though the sound of their laughter followed him for a good many yards.

George Friar was not yet here. He'd hoped to have a word with him, not to warn him off exactly, but to allow the colonial to understand the danger of becoming involved in political intrigues against England. Still, Gabriel was prepared to wait, and it was early.

A hundred pounds later Gabriel acknowledged his mind was not on the game and cashed in his chips.

'Thank you, gentlemen, but that is me out for the evening.'

Francis St Cartmail pulled his substantial winnings over in front of him. 'Are you sure you will not stay, Gabriel? I could do with as much as you can lose.'

For the first time that evening Gabriel smiled as if he meant it. 'Daniel and Luce are out there somewhere. Get them to sit down with you.'

The other shook his head. 'Ross is skint and Montcliffe is a responsible married man. He spends his extra on the horses he sees with potential and, by God, he is doing well with it, too.'

'You can't get in on the game?'

'Never really interested, I am afraid. But I am off to the Americas in a month or so on the search for gold.'

'You think you will find some?' A fresh spurt of interest surged.

'I do. Come with me. I'd be happy to have you along.'

The invitation was both sincere and unexpected and Gabriel thought that if he had not been consumed in his revenge for Henrietta's death he might have even taken him up on it.

'I met a man a few months back who told me to look for gold in North Carolina, Francis. He said the town of Concord was the place I should journey to and his brother-in-law, Samuel Huie, was the man who would show me where to look. He said Huie had found a nugget as big as his fist while he was out fishing one day. As he did not seem like a man who often embellished the truth, I believed the yarn.'

'Well, I will keep the information in mind and if I find it in the place you mention, I will keep bring some back for you.'

'Then I wish you all the luck in the world.'

'Thank you for the dance, Miss Ashfield.' Mr George Friar's words were laced with a slight

American accent as he drew Adelaide to one side of the room. 'Are you enjoying your time here in London?'

'Indeed, sir.' This was a complete lie, but she knew if she had said otherwise she would have a complicated explanation in front of her.

'I saw you speaking with Lord Wesley the other night at the Bradfords' ball. Is he a particular friend of yours?'

Unexpectedly the blood rushed to her face and Adelaide cursed her reaction, especially when she saw the man's obvious curiosity.

'I am newly come to London, Mr Friar. I barely know the earl.'

'But you have heard the stories, no doubt? He is not to be trusted and it would be wise for any woman to keep her distance.'

Such a confidence made Adelaide shiver.

'A strong opinion, sir. Is he an acquaintance of yours?'

The man shook his head. 'No, but he led the wife of my cousin astray and it cost her her life, an ending she did not in any way deserve.'

'You are implying then some sense of blame

on the part of Lord Wesley, sir?' She had made a point of asking Lucy and her other acquaintances here about the chequered past of Gabriel Hughes since meeting him, partly out of interest, but mostly out of the feeling he was somehow being wrongly dealt to. She could not explain her connection with a man who appeared to be everything she had always abhorred and yet... 'From the stories I have heard it was your cousin's wife who had absconded with her lover in the first place?'

This time Friar laughed out loud. 'A woman who is not afraid to voice all that she thinks is a rare jewel in the London court. Why are you not married ten times over already, Miss Ashfield? Can these English lords not recognise a veritable treasure when they see one?'

She brushed off his nonsense though a part of her was pleased at such praise. 'A woman's need for a husband is overrated in my opinion, though my uncle is not to be persuaded otherwise.'

For a moment his visage was one of shock before he managed to drag his expression back.

'Well, Miss Ashfield, I have always applauded

honesty in a woman. Would you take a walk with me, perchance, so that I might tell you a story?'

Adelaide looked around. She could see Lord Berrick making his way towards her and wanted to avoid him.

'Perhaps a turn on the terrace for privacy might be in order.' Friar said this as he saw where she looked.

She did not wish to be alone with Mr Friar, she thought, remembering Lord Wesley's warning, but glancing through the glass she observed others lingering there and enjoying the unusual balminess of the evening.

It could not hurt for five minutes to listen to what he had to say, surely, and with the growing warmth in the room she would appreciate a little fresh air.

Once outside Adelaide could tell Mr Friar was trying to think up what words to give her next as he looked over the small balustrade leading into the garden. Finally he spoke.

'There are some who would say that the Earl of Wesley is not the fop he pretends to be. My cousin, for example, was completely crushed by the loss of his precious wife. He does not believe her demise was an accident at all.'

'What does he believe, then?'

'If I could speak plainly, I would say he thinks Wesley killed her for he had become tired of her neediness as his lover and wanted her gone.'

Shock ran through Adelaide at the bitterness in his words and also that such an accusation should be levelled at Gabriel Hughes. 'Presumably the courts thought otherwise, Mr Friar, as I heard there was a case of law to be answered for it.' The thought did cross her mind as to why she should be such a stalwart in her defence of a man whose reputation was hardly pristine, given everything she knew of Lord Wesley had come through gossip.

'Indeed they did, Miss Ashfield, but justice and money walk hand in hand and the Wesley title holds its own sway in such decisions.'

'Such are the words of those who perceive their case lost by some unfair disadvantage that they can never prove. Better to move on and make your life over than look back and wreak havoc with all that is left.'

'You are not the more normal sort of débutante, Miss Ashfield, with your strong opinions.'

'I will take that as a compliment, Mr Friar, for I am older and a lot wiser. Wise enough to know that people can say anything of anyone and yet the saying of it does not make it true.'

He laughed, but the sound was not pleasant. 'Have you ever been to the Americas?'

When she shook her head he continued.

'I own a large property in Baltimore, in Coles Harbor on the west side of the Jones Falls River. I have come to England to find a partner who might enjoy the place with me, neither a timid bride, Miss Ashfield, nor a young one. I need a woman who would cope with the rigours of the New World and one with enough of a fortune to help me build my own legacy.'

'I see.' And Adelaide suddenly did. She had left the relative safety of the frying pan that was Lord Berrick and jumped into a fire.

It was how the business of marriage worked in London, after all, brides were only a commodity and an article of trade. Men put their collateral on the table and a prudent woman weighed up her options and accepted the most favourable. For life. For ever. It was exactly as Aunt Eloise had said it would be, was it not? Women sold their souls for marriage and regretted it until the end of time.

The thought of it all held her mute, but George Friar seemed to have taken her silence as acquiescence, for he leaned forward and took her fingers in his own before his lips came down hard upon the back of them.

Cold, wet and grasping. She could not believe he would dare to touch her like this out here amongst others, but as she broke away and looked around she realised everybody on this end of the terrace had left to go inside.

Mr Friar hadn't released her, either, his fingers still entwined in hers and allowing no means of escape, the expression on his face ardent as he breathed out rapidly.

'Oh, come now, Miss Ashfield, I am certain we could do better than that. You look like a woman with a great deal of sensuality about you and, if I say so myself, I am considered something of a catch by the unmarried women of Baltimore.

A new life, an adventure and the opportunity to use your considerable fortune in a way that could double it again. Take the chance of it whilst you can. Caution can be most stultifying.'

Adelaide thought quickly. She needed to diffuse this situation and get back inside without causing even more of a scene. 'I am sure you are as you say, sir, a veritable catch, but believe me when I tell you that I have no want for a husband despite my presence here.' This explanation solved nothing, however, for his grip tightened as he pulled her towards him. 'I will ask you one more time to please let me go, sir.' She hated the slight shiver in her words as he met her glance directly and lifted his brows. A game? He thought it such?

'One kiss, then, to convince you. Surely that would not be amiss?'

The sharp slap of fingers on his cheek and his legs caught on the edge of a pot plant tipping him off balance. Even as she reached forward to stop him tumbling he was gone, falling over the balustrade in an ungainly surprise and lying prone and motionless on the path below.

My God, had she killed him? Forgetting about convention and her own safety, she scrambled down after him and saw in relief that he still breathed.

She could hardly just leave him here, but to do otherwise would involve her in discussions she would rather not be a part of. A movement from above surprised her, but she knew who it was immediately.

Chapter Four

'We meet again, Miss Ashfield.'

'In circumstances even more trying than the last time, I am afraid, Lord Wesley. Mr Friar is newly come from the Americas and seems to have a poor understanding of the word "no". His ability to pretend to be something he is not must be the only thing allowing him entrance here for he has few other redeeming features.' She knew she was babbling, but couldn't seem to stop. Surprise and relief at the earl's presence obliterated her more normal reason and fright had made her shake.

As he joined her, Gabriel Hughes placed two fingers across the pulse on George Friar's neck. 'A trifle fast, but given the circumstances...'

Today he looked tired, the darkened skin beneath both eyes alluding to a lack of sleep. His glance had also taken in the telltale mark on the unconscious man's cheek.

'His dress sense is appalling, would you not say?'

At that she smiled. There was a certain sang-froid apparent in the comment. Indeed, he did not look even the least perturbed about what had happened.

'I didn't push him. He fell across that potted plant and down into the garden.'

'After you slapped him?'

She felt her own blood rise. 'I had asked him to remove his hand from my person, Lord Wesley, and he did not.'

He looked up quickly. 'He didn't hurt you?' His gold eyes were darker tonight, though when she shook her head the anger in them softened.

'Perhaps then it would be better if you were gone when he awakes?'

Taking that as a hint, she turned.

'Miss Ashfield?'

She turned back. 'Yes?'

'If you say nothing of this to anyone, I will make certain that he never does, either.'

'How?' The question tumbled out in horror.

'A firm threat is what I was thinking, but if you want him dead…?'

Could he possibly mean what she thought he did? Friar's explanation of how Wesley had killed Henrietta tumbled in her mind to be dismissed as the upturn of his lips held her spellbound. He was teasing, but already she could hear the voices of others coming closer and knew she needed to be gone. Still she could not quite leave it at that.

'Sometimes I am not certain about just exactly who you are, my lord. Amongst the pomp and splendour of your clothes and the artful tie of your cravat I detect a man who is not quite the one that he appears.'

But Gabriel Hughes shook his head. 'It would be much safer for you to view me exactly as the rest of the world does, Miss Ashfield; a dissolute and licentious earl without a care for anything save the folds in his most complicated cravat.'

No humour lingered now, the hard planes of

his face intractable, and as George Friar groaned Adelaide fled. She could not fathom the Earl of Wesley at all and that was the trouble. He was nothing like any man she had met before. Even when he laughed the danger in him was observable and clear. But the colour of his eyes in this light was that of the gilded hawks she'd seen as a young girl in a travelling menagerie that had visited Sherborne, the quiet strength in them hidden under humour.

Lady Harcourt looked up as she came to her side. 'You are always disappearing, my dear. I am certain that is not a trait to be greatly encouraged. If your uncle were here and he asked me of your whereabouts, I would not know, you see, and so it would be far better if...'

Her words petered off as a shout at one end of the salon had them turning and Adelaide saw Mr Friar burst into the room using a large white handkerchief to wipe off his bleeding nose. She was glad he was heading straight for the exit even as she stepped back into the shadow of her chaperon.

Gabriel Hughes came into view behind him,

accompanied by Lord Montcliffe, and the Earl of Wesley's left hand was buried deep in his pocket. Walking together, the two men were of a similar height and build and every feminine eye of the *ton* was trained towards them as well as a good many of the masculine ones.

'Goodness me. What is society coming to these days?' Lady Harcourt lifted her lorgnette to her face to get a better view. 'A fist fight in the middle of a crowded ball? Who is that short man, Bertram, with Lord Wesley and Lord Montcliffe?'

Adelaide's heart began to beat fast and then faster. Would there be a scene? Would she be revealed as the perpetrator of the American's questionable condition?

'Mr George Friar is an arrogant cheat,' her cousin drawled. 'Perhaps the Earl of Wesley has finally done what many of the others here have not been able to.'

'What?' Imelda's voice was censorious. 'Broken his nose?'

'Nay, Aunt. Shut him up.'

The Earl of Berrick, standing beside them,

frowned. 'I have my doubts that Lord Wesley would put himself out for such a one unless it suited his purpose.'

Bertie nodded in agreement. 'He'd be far more likely to be in the card room or cavorting with the numerous women of the *ton* who are unhappy in their marriages.'

Lady Harcourt gave her grand-nephew a stern look. 'You are in the company of a young girl in her first Season, Bertram. Please mind your tongue.'

'Pardon me, Aunt, and I am sorry, Addie.'

Her cousin gave her one of the smiles that Adelaide could never ever resist.

'Make it up to me, then.'

'How.'

'Come with me as my chaperon to the Royal Botanic Gardens at Kew. There is a physic garden there that I have always wanted to see.'

'You look like hell, Gabe.' Daniel Wylde did not mince his words as they left the Harveys' ball. 'You need some beauty sleep.'

Gabriel heard the concern behind the words. 'I'll live.'

'Who was he, to you? Mr Friar back there?'

'No one. He'd tripped over the balustrade and had fallen. I was the first to find him.'

'I doubt that.' Montcliffe's words were low. 'Unless you have taken to slapping strange men I would say there was a woman involved. Besides, you would hardly take a hard swipe at an injured man unless you had some gripe with him?'

Gabriel swore, but didn't answer.

'Your sister, Charlotte, was unkind, Gabriel, but you were always nicer.'

'It's been a while. People change. I'd be the first to admit that I have.'

'Why?'

One word biting at his guts, so easy just to spill the worries and feel better. Even easier to not. Still it might not hurt to sound Montcliffe out on a little of it.

'What do you know of Randolph Clements?'

'His wife, Henrietta, died in the fire at Raven-shill Chapel. It was rumoured you had something to do with that, but it was never proven.'

'I think Clements killed his wife.'

'And walked away?'

'Unconvicted. Mr Friar here is one of his American cousins.'

'You think he was involved, too?'

'Odds are that he is here in London for a reason.'

'He is single and wealthy. He wants a wife. Many might say that is enough of a reason. Who slapped him before you turned up?'

'Miss Adelaide Ashfield.'

'And she is…?'

Gabriel swallowed hard. 'Penbury's niece and one of this Season's débutantes.'

'The woman in gold?' Montcliffe began to smile. 'God, you have an interest in this lady.'

'No.' He made the word sound as definite as he could.

'Yet you just avenged her for an insult, I am presuming? Such an action indicates more than mere indifference.'

Gabriel had forgotten about Daniel Wylde's quick mind. He could also see the wheels of curiosity turning in sharp eyes.

'You never told me about happened in the

bloody chapel? Some say it was you who lit the fire.'

'No, I can't even remember how it started. I know I did try to save her, but then...' He stopped, searching for a glimpse into recall and failing.

'You couldn't?'

'I didn't love Henrietta Clements in the way she wanted me to.'

There was silence, the guilt of it all howling around the edges of Gabriel's sanity like a cold wind blowing relentlessly from the north. He had had liaisons with women all of his adult life, un-requited political connections, and this was the result. His penance. His atonement. The result-ing impotence was only deserved and proper. A God-given punishment so very close to the cause of all his destruction—he could not deny it.

If he had been alone he might have hit some-thing, but he wasn't. As it was he held his hands into the side of his thighs in tight fists. The nail on his right forefinger broke into the skin of his thumb.

'Perhaps I hurt your sister in the same way?' Daniel offered the explanation.

'Pardon?' With all his other thoughts Gabriel could not quite work out exactly what was meant.

'Charlotte. I didn't love her enough, either, and we ruined each other. Same thing you are talking of, isn't it?'

The minutes of quiet multiplied.

'But then Amethyst taught me about the honesty of love.'

God, Gabriel thought, *and what I would not give for a wife like that.* Empty loneliness curled into the corners of hope. He had never felt close to anyone and now it would never again be possible.

For a second he almost hated the other's joy. It was what happened when you were down on your luck. You became surrounded by those who were not. Even his sister, for all her poor choices in life, had written to say that she had met a wealthy and cultured man in Edinburgh with whom she could see a future.

'Come to Montcliffe, Gabe. Some country air might be just what you need. Amethyst is almost eight months along in her pregnancy so she does not come to London any more, preferring the quiet of Montcliffe.' Daniel Wylde was watching him closely. 'She would be pleased to have you there and so would I.'

Thanking him for the offer, Gabriel replied that he would certainly think about it and then he left.

He actually spent the night thinking of Adelaide Ashfield. Her smile. Her blue eyes. The quiet lisp in her words. Friar was a threat to her in some way he could not as yet fathom. Gabriel knew that he was. He returned his attention to the notes spread across the table in front of him—maps, drawings and timings—as he searched for a pattern.

Clements was there somewhere in the middle of the puzzle though he had been careful to cover his tracks. His cousin George Friar told others that he had arrived in England a month or so before Henrietta had died, on the clipper *Vigilant* travelling between Baltimore and London. But when he had tracked down the passenger list for that particular voyage his name had not been upon it. Why would he lie about such a thing? Had he lied about who he was as well?

Frank Richardson had visited Friar and Clements, too. He had stayed over at the Whitehorse Tavern with John Goode, his cousin.

Four of them now. Gabriel knew there were six, because Henrietta Clements had told him so. She had been so angry she could barely talk when she had come to him at Ravenshill, that much he did remember.

'My husband is here,' she had said simply. 'Right behind me, and I know for certain his political allegiances lie with France and Napoleon's hopes. Take me away to the Americas, Gabriel. I have an aunt who lives there. In Boston. We could be free to begin again…together, for I have money I can access and much in the way of jewellery.' Her arms came around him even as he tried to move away.

Then there was blankness, an empty space of time without memory. He had been trying to fill in the details ever since, but the only true and residing certainty he'd kept was the pain.

The knock at the door was expected, but still

he stood to one side of the jamb and called out, 'Who is it?'

'Archie McCrombie, sir.' The reply was firm.

Sliding the latch downwards, Gabriel ushered the small red-haired man inside, the cold air of evening blowing in with him and his coat lifting in the wind.

'Friar is residing at Beaumont Street, where he has spent most of the last week enjoying the charms of Mrs Fitzgerald's girls. I left Ben there to make certain he stays put.'

'Did he meet anyone else?'

'Frank Richardson, my lord. I did not recognise the others who came and went. Someone tailed me as I left, but I shook him off. Tall he was and well dressed. He does not seem to fit in around this side of town. He was armed, too, I would bet my life on the fact.'

'Expecting trouble, then, or about to cause it?'

'Both, I would say, sir. I'd have circled back and tailed him, my lord, if I wasnna meeting you.'

'No, you did well. Give them some rope to

hang themselves; we don't just want one fish, we want all six of them.'

'Yes, sir.'

After McCrombie left, Gabriel stood and walked to the window. It was raining outside and grey and the cold enveloped him, his life worn down into a shadow of what it had previously been.

His finances were shaky. He had gone through his accounts again and again, trying to find a way to cut down his spending, but his country estate of Ravenshill was bleeding out money as was his London town house. He wasn't down to the last of his cash yet, as Daniel Wylde had been, but give it a few more years and...

He shook that thought away.

Once he had those associated with Clements he could leave London and retreat to Ravenshill Manor. Then he would sell off the town house. The new trading classes were always on the lookout for an old and aristocratic residence in the right location and he knew it would go quickly. In Essex he would be able to manage at least until his mother was no longer with him. He shook that thought away and swore softly as he remembered back to their conversation at dinner the night before.

'You need to find a wife who would give you children, Gabriel. You would be much happier then.'

The anger that had been so much a part of him since the fire burgeoned. 'I doubt I will ever marry.'

The tight skin on his right thigh underlined all that he now wasn't. No proper women would have him in the state he was in and even courtesans and prostitutes were out of his reach. A no-man's lad. A barren and desolate void.

When his mother reached out to place her hand over his he had felt both her warmth and her age. Her melancholy was getting worse, but he did not mention that as he tried to allay her fears.

'Everything will work out. We will leave London soon and go up to Essex. You can start a garden and read. Perhaps even take up the piano again?'

Tears had welled in the old and opaque eyes. 'I named you for the angel from the Bible, you know, Gabriel, and I was right to, but sometimes now I think there is only sadness left…'

Her words had tapered off and he shook his head to stop her from saying more, the teachings of the ancient shepherd of Hermas coming to mind.

'In regard of faith there are two angels within man. One of Righteousness and one of Iniquity.'

The Angel of Iniquity was a better analogy to describe himself now, Gabriel thought, but refrained from telling her so.

The sum of his life. Wrathful. Bitter. Foolish. Cut off. Even Alan Wolfe, the Director of the British Service, had stated that Gabriel could no longer serve in the same capacity he had done, his profile after the fire too high for a department cloaked in secrecy.

So he had kept on at it largely alone, day after day and week after week. A more personal revenge. Once he had thought the emotion a negative one, but now…?

It was like a drug, creeping through his bones and shattering all that was dull; a questionable integrity, he knew that, but nevertheless his own.

The veneer of social insouciance was becoming harder and harder to maintain, the light and airy manners of a fop overlaying a heavy coat of steel. The lacy shirt cuffs, the carefully tied cravat. A smile where only fury lingered and an ever-increasing solitude.

Adelaide Ashfield's honesty had shaken him, made him think, her directness piercing all that he had hoped to hide and so very easily. But there were things that she was not telling him, either, he could see this was so in the unguarded depths of those blue eyes. And Friar was circling around her, his derogatory evaluation of England's royal family and its Parliament as much of a topic of his every conversation as his need to make a good marriage.

Revolution came from deprivation and loss, and he could not for the life of him work out why George Friar, a successful Baltimore businessman by his own account, would throw in his lot with the unpopular anti-British sentiments of his cousin. They were blood-related, but they were also wildly different people.

Perhaps it was in the pursuit of a religious

fervour he had come with, the whispers of the young prince's depravities rising. America's independence had the same ring of truth to it, there was no doubt about that, a better way of living, a more equitable society and one unhampered by a monarch without scruples.

Conjecture and distrust. This is what his life had come to now, Gabriel thought, for he seldom took people at their face value any more, but looked for the dark blackness of their souls.

Gabriel strained to remember the laughter inside the words of Miss Adelaide Ashfield as he poured himself a drink, hating the way his hands shook when he raised the crystal decanter.

She was the first person he had ever met who seemed true and real and genuine, artifice and dissimulation a thousand miles from her honestly given opinions.

But he did wonder just who the hell had hurt her.

Chapter Five

Adelaide had tried to like Frederick Lovelace, the Earl of Berrick, but in truth he was both boring and vain, two vices that added together led to the third one of shallowness.

'A titled aristocrat no less,' her uncle had proclaimed after noticing Berrick's interest at their last meeting, a lilt in his voice and pride in his step. 'I thought Richard Williams a catch, but here is a man of ten thousand pounds a year, my dear, and a country home that is the envy of all who see it.'

As the earl in question regaled her with myriad facts about horse racing, however, Adelaide struggled to feign an interest.

Eventually he came to the end of his soliloquy and stopped. 'Do you enjoy horses, Miss Ashfield?' he queried, finally mindful of the fact that he had not asked one question that pertained to her as yet.

'No. I generally try to stay well away from them, my lord.' She saw the resulting frown of Lady Harcourt and her uncle as he began to speak.

'My niece rides, of course, though the tutor I employed to teach the finer points found her timid. Perhaps you might take a turn together in Hyde Park if it suited you. I think she simply needs more practice at the sport to become proficient at it.

'Indeed, if you were going there by any chance today, perhaps we could meet, Miss Ashfield? I should be more than willing to help in your equestrian education.'

Her uncle looked pleased and nodded with pride. 'Well, now that you mention it we were intending to take a turn around the park.'

Adelaide did not deign to answer, but her pulse began to race. Please God that her uncle would not promise Berrick her company.

'Perhaps my niece and I could meet you there around five?'

Short of refusing outright Adelaide could say nothing. At least her uncle would be with her, but it was just this sort of ridiculousness that had put her off coming to London right from the beginning.

'I shall be there at five, then. Lord Penbury, Miss Ashfield.' Taking her hand as everyone stood, Berrick bowed across it, his head barely reaching the top of her brow and a growing bald patch clearly visible.

When he was gone her uncle finished the last of the brandy in his glass and turned towards her.

'A well brought-up young man, I think, Adelaide. A man who might suit you well with his wide interests and great fortune. At least we would know it is not your money that he is after for he is well endowed with his own.'

Adelaide listened with horror. 'You promised you would allow me the choice of a husband should I come for the Season, Uncle. I should not wish to be told who is the right one to choose and who is not.'

'That might all be very well, my love, but Frederick Lovelace is a good man from a sterling family and it behoves me as your uncle to offer the advice so that you are aware he'd make a remarkable connection.'

'He may be a good man, Uncle, but he is not the good man for me.'

Alec Ashfield turned and for the first time ever Adelaide saw real anger come into his eyes. 'Then find one, my dear. Find a man who can be all that you need and want and I will give you my blessing.'

Lady Harcourt stood as tension filled the room about them.

'I am sure she will, Alec. It may just take a little time for your niece to realise the honour the Earl of Berrick accords her, but let us hope this meeting you have organised goes somewhere towards the fact.'

Adelaide took her leave, feeling like screaming all the way up to her room on the second floor. She should never have agreed to come to London in the first place, she knew that now. She should have stayed at Sherborne and dug her feet in, refusing to be budged by any argument presented, because this was the result of it all. This coercion and well-meaning forcefulness.

When a tear welled up and fell over one cheek she angrily wiped it away.

She had not always needed to explain things to her old aunts, the fact that she was resigned to a productive spinsterhood simply accepted. An option the same as the one they themselves had taken and nary a second of regret for it, either.

The day suddenly felt heavy and difficult and now there was the further worry of a ride in a few hours in Hyde Park with a suitor who had a lot more hope than she knew was warranted. Could she feign sickness and simply miss it? She shook her head.

No, she would meet the Earl of Berrick with her uncle and tell him herself that she was not interested in marrying him or anybody at all. Hopefully that would be the end of it.

The ride began badly as Lord Berrick took her hand and pressed his lips to her skin, an action so reminiscent of her skirmish with Mr Friar that she found herself snatching her fingers back and standing there speechless. All around her others watched, the eyes of the *ton* upon them.

'I have looked forward to this, Miss Ashfield. I hope you will allow me to help you mount.'

When he placed his hands beneath the stirrup of the horse Adelaide thanked him. At least up on her steed he would be out of touch, so to speak, and she might be able to relax just a little.

She and her uncle had dismounted as soon as they had got inside the gates and now her uncle had elected to stay and wait whilst she took a turn about Rotten Row. This was a tactical manoeuvre, probably, and one that gave Frederick Lovelace some time alone with her.

At least the track was busy. With only a small difficulty she could get around the whole thing without having to converse with him to a great extent save to tell him of her desire to remain unattached.

Adelaide had never been proficient at managing a horse and here amongst many other steeds her stallion seemed nervy and difficult. At Northbridge she seldom rode, preferring instead to walk the short distances between the manor and the village. In London it seemed everybody was an expert, the tooling precise and accomplished.

Taking in a breath, she tried to hide a building fear. She had heard it mentioned more than once that horses could tell if their rider was afraid and acted accordingly. From the prancing of the horse beneath her she was sure he must understand her frame of mind completely. It obviously felt a certain attraction for the filly the Earl of Berrick rode, as it constantly veered to one side to get closer.

Just what she needed, she thought to herself, and, jamming her hand about the reins, made a supreme effort to keep them apart. At that moment when she looked up she stared straight into the laughing molten glance of Lord Wesley.

'Miss Ashfield.' He tipped his hat to her. The animal he rode was huge and black. A mount she imagined one would ride into battle, the arrogant stance of its head marking it out as different from all the others in the park.

Like horse, like owner, she found herself thinking uncharitably, though his presence seemed to have had the effect of making Lord Berrick back off a bit and for that she was glad. Two more turns and she could reasonably call it a day. If she managed one with Lord Wesley then all the better.

'I see you are as proficient at riding as you are at dancing the waltz.'

She could not help but smile. 'You have not yet seen me paint a watercolour or stitch a tapestry. I am even worse at those most necessary of feminine skills.'

When he laughed the sound burrowed down into the marrow of her bones, making her warmer than she had been.

'What are you good at, then?' he asked.

'Healing,' she returned. 'I run a clinic at Northbridge and people come for miles to get my ointments and tinctures. I have a garden, you see, and my aunts taught me many things about—'

She stopped as she saw his surprise and wondered if such skills would be deemed appropriate by the lords and ladies of society.

'Like Asclepius?' he returned and she shook her head.

'Well, I cannot restore the dead to the living as he did, my lord, but then neither do I wish to be smote with Zeus's thunder.'

'It might be argued accepting gold for raising the dead was hardly good form. Someone had to stop it.'

Adelaide was astonished. It was seldom she had met anyone, apart from her aged aunts, with a solid memory for the complicated names and deeds of the Grecian legends. A scholar, then, and a man who hid such learning? Today the sun had brought out the colour in his hair to a variety of shades of light brown, red and gold. When he wiped back the unruly hair on his forehead, she saw that the knuckles on his left hand were bruised and split. From the contretemps with Friar?

Adelaide glanced about to see that Lord Berrick was not too close before she mentioned them. 'I could give you salve for your fingers if you wanted it.'

As an answer to that he merely jammed his

hand into his pocket and she pushed back her spectacles with a sigh.

'Why do you wear them?' He did not sound happy.

'The spectacles?' She couldn't quite understand what he meant.

'The glass in them is plain. Poor eyesight normally requires the fashioning of a lens for improved vision.'

She gave back her own question. 'Do you keep hawks, my lord?'

'No. Why?' He shifted on his horse in order to watch her better.

'I think you would hold an affinity with a bird who notices all that is around him even as he pretends nonchalance.'

With a gentlemanly tilt of his head Gabriel Hughes dropped back; a slight tug on the leather and he was gone, Lovelace replacing him.

'Is it not just the most appealing time of day, Miss Ashfield, and might I also say that you ride magnificently.'

As Adelaide swallowed back mirth she also

resisted the strong impulse to turn around and look for the enigmatic Earl of Wesley.

Gabriel watched her trot on with the popinjay Lovelace chattering beside her and thought he should simply turn for the gate and leave. But something made him stay. Her uncertainty with the horse, he was to think later, or the unguarded way she had looked at him when she had offered her salve.

The shout came from close by, reverberating as a young man called his friend. Any other day such a sound might not have mattered, but with Adelaide holding her reins so tightly her horse took umbrage and reared. She had no hope at all in managing it.

Berrick simply stepped his horse to the side and watched, uncertain as to what he could do.

Gabriel was off his mount in a second and strode towards her frightened animal, reaching out for the dangling reins as he told Adelaide Ashfield to hold on any way that she could. Frightened blue eyes turned to him, but the message seemed to be getting across as she crouched down on the back of the stallion and grabbed large handfuls of mane in her fists.

Within a moment he had gentled the horse, and when it had settled enough for Gabriel to move around to the side, he reached up to the terrified rider.

'You can let go now. I have you.'

Her fingers seemed frozen and he unfolded her fists before taking her waist and sliding her from the horse. Letting her go as soon as she was on the ground, he was glad someone had come forward to hold the reins.

'You're safe. I promise.'

'Th-thank y-you.' Breathless and shaking, Adelaide found her hair had half fallen from its pins and her hat was missing. The trembling had worsened.

'I…I never l-liked horses and they d-don't like me, either. I sh-should have just walked.'

'And missed an adventure? At least you didn't let the stallion unseat you. Landing on your bottom in the middle of a busy park might be more cause for consternation.'

At that she smiled and brought up the back of

her hand to wipe away the tears. She still felt shocked, but his humour was normalising every-thing and making her feel less panicked.

Her uncle had reached them now, too, and he grasped her arm in a tight hold.

'I saw what happened. Are you hurt?'

'No, I th-think I am f-fine.' Alec Ashfield's at-tention shifted to Gabriel Hughes.

'Lord Wesley.' Frosty and cold. 'Thank you for your help, but I can manage things from here.'

'Of course, Lord Penbury.'

The chill in the earl's voice was noticeable as he stepped back, leading his horse away as the gathering crowd allowed him a passage out.

She wanted to cry. She did. She wanted to run after Gabriel Hughes and hold on to his safety and protection. She wanted him to tell her that everything was all right in that particular dry humour of his that made her feel…special.

Lord Berrick took the place vacated by Ga-briel Hughes. 'I would have managed your horse, Miss Ashfield, but Wesley had already jumped into the fray. I did not realise that you were so inexperienced or I would never have suggested such an outing and now I am afraid your dress is ruined and your hat is quite flattened. At least your spectacles are not broken and that is something we can be well thankful for...'

Even her uncle watched Lovelace with a sort of disbelief as he babbled on, stopping only as Bertram hurried across.

'My God, Wesley is a hero,' he exclaimed, admiration apparent in every word. 'If he had not dragged your mount to stillness the way he did, Addie, you would have been thrown from its back, and with an animal that size it's a long way down.'

'Quite.' Her uncle's voice was as tight as the expression on Lovelace's face.

'I hope someone thanked him?' Bertram continued on, seemingly unaware of the atmosphere. 'For his shoulder muscles will be sore from the tugging, there is no doubt of that.'

Adelaide smiled. Her cousin was such a dear sometimes despite his gambling and drinking.

'Perhaps we were not quite as effusive as we might have been,' her uncle said quietly. 'I will send a note to Wesley when we get home.'

Home.

The whole episode had left Adelaide exhausted and she was glad when her uncle and cousin took charge of the horses and they headed the short distance towards the town house on Grosvenor Square.

Once she had bathed and dressed and her stomach had settled Adelaide took her large leather bag from the wardrobe and opened the flap.

She seldom went anywhere without all her oils and salves and tinctures. They grounded her and relaxed her in a way nothing else did, and she liked the weight of the mortar and pestle in her hand.

A healing salve was an easy thing to make. Gathering up an amber bottle of herbs infused in oil, she poured out a generous amount. Arnica for bruising and calendula for the abrasions. The smell of comfrey and duckweed made her breathe in, their properties of knitting the skin together and soothing irritation welcomed.

As her small burner flamed she heated beeswax on a very low temperature and added that to her mix. Lavender was placed in last, the smell pungent and masculine.

Choosing a little container of bright-green glass, she poured the salve into it and did the lid up. Around the side Adelaide twisted a thick tie of string and added a stalk of lavender.

Finished.

Taking a sheet of paper from her armoire, she wrapped it, placing a note inside. She had no idea as to where the earl lived, but, calling in her uncle's butler, instructed him with the task of seeing that the parcel reached Lord Gabriel Wesley as quickly as it was able.

The package arrived after a late supper, brought by a minion of the Penbury household who was under strict instructions to place the offering directly into his hands.

'Miss Ashfield says it will spoil otherwise. She said it would need to be used across the next few days to be at its most potent, my lord.'

'Very well.' Gabriel waited till the servant was gone and shut the door behind him. A strong smell of lavender came from the parcel.

Crossing to his desk, he opened the gift and pulled out a small green jar that had been tightly shut, a sprig of the same flower wrapped into the side. A note fluttered from the bottom of the glass, held on by a dob of red wax.

Lord Wesley,
Thank you for your help today in the park.
As you were quick to point out I should prob-
ably be suffering from bad bruising if you
had not saved me.

But it has come to my attention that the
same might not be said for you. I sincerely
hope that the abrasions on your hand have
not been worsened by such a kindness.

This is a healing salve. Place it across your
damaged skin once at night and then again
in the morning. It would work well on any
tender muscles as well. I am sure you will
notice the difference.
Yours sincerely
Miss Adelaide Ashfield

Gabriel could not help but smile. His knuckles were barely wounded compared to all the other hurts he had suffered. But she had thought of him and acted upon it; a gesture that was appreciated and unexpected.

Scooping out some of the ointment, he was surprised to feel the coolness of it on his skin. Beneath the scent of lavender other smells lingered, but he did not have the expertise to identify them. Comfrey, he thought. He had smelt that after the fire in some of the salves applied to his leg and would never forget it. He wondered if the mixture would ease the tightness of the scarring on his thighs as well and decided to try it when he went to bed.

He had never really had a gift before, delivered to him and wrapped in flowers and scent. Oh, he had given small trinkets to paramours across the years, but he had not received gifts back and his own family had seldom bothered with Christmas and birthdays.

Too busy trying to simply survive with a father who was often angry. When Geoffrey Hughes had been killed in a tavern brawl in London those left had breathed a sigh of relief.

Thirteen had been an impressionable age to

lose a parent and whilst he had become difficult, his sister had changed into a wild thing almost overnight.

No wonder his mother had barely coped before slipping into a melancholy that hadn't left her.

The wreck of his family had been allayed a few years later by the warm arms of willing lovers and there had been a long line pleased to allow him succour. But no longer.

Bringing his hand to his nose, Gabriel inhaled deeply; the smell of goodness and healing and Adelaide Ashfield was comforting. He wished she had come herself to deliver the gifts.

Chapter Six

After her fright in the park Uncle Alec and Lady Harcourt did not press her into any social engagements the next morning. Indeed, they left the day up to her discretion entirely and when Adelaide expressed an interest in visiting Lackington, Allen and Co. at their Temple of the Muses shop in Finsbury Square, her uncle readied a carriage to take her.

Today accompanied only by her maid Adelaide felt freer than she had done in weeks. The muscles at the top of her arms hurt a little from her tussle with the horse yesterday, but all in all the trade-off was a good one.

With the sky blue above and the air fresh around her she stopped in front of the facade of the shop and looked up. A flag waved on top of a large dome and in the distance she could hear the sound of bells.

Aunt Jean and Aunt Eloise had often spoken of this place in hushed tones. They had told stories of the number of books for sale here and of the generosity of Lackington's prices. Adelaide could not wait to see it for herself.

Inside was as prepossessing as it had been without, the rows of books arranged in cyclical order all the way into the ceiling and a good many men and women were browsing what was on offer.

After asking the man at the desk where to find a book on English plant life, she was directed to a less busy part of the building with rows of promising-looking tomes before her.

Milly was delighted when Adelaide assured her it would be most proper for her maid to go on her own search of things to read. She had taught the girl her letters at Northbridge and knew she would enjoy the chance to find her particular favourites.

Forty minutes later and with a large pile of books in her arms Adelaide went searching for somewhere to sit. Turning a corner promising quiet, she came upon the Earl of Wesley reading at one of the private tables.

He did not look at all pleased to see her, a heavy frown marring his forehead, though it did nothing to diminish his beauty.

'Miss Ashfield.'

His reading material seemed to consist mainly of shipping routes and maps, but she did notice a few volumes that looked surprisingly like the botanicals she herself had chosen.

Almost furtively he laid a paper down on top of them. She wondered what he could be doing with a tome of medical botany by William Woodville outlining diseases of the body and the newest possible cures.

'I did not expect to see you here, my lord.' Her glance dropped to the skin on his knuckles. The wounds appeared to be considerably better than yesterday.

'Because you imagined the gambling halls to be more to my taste?' He had regained his humour quickly, but today there was also another emotion that she had not seen there before.

Wariness. It sat upon his face, ambushing the more normal indifference.

'I hope the salve I sent you was of some use.'

As he glanced down at his hand he spoke slowly. 'It was. The bruising is almost gone.'

'That will be the arnica, I expect, and the dash of vinegar. Keep applying the ointment for two more days each morning and night. It is at its most effective fresh, but should keep for at least a few months if you make certain the lid is tight and that it is stored out of the direct sunlight.'

'You are skilled at what you do, Miss Ashfield.'

'You believed I would not be?'

'I am not truly certain what to believe of you. A woman of science and healing. A débutante who is here for the Season and yet eschews the promise of Holy Matrimony. A lady who fails to see any sort of a need for women to excel in painting, dancing or tapestry. But obviously an avid reader of botanicals and the art of medicinal healing. And romance?' His eyes caught the slender volumes at the bottom of her pile.

But two could play at this game and Adelaide was well up to the task. She squared her jaw.

'And what of you, my lord? Routes of long-distance shipping lines and maps of the English countryside. And botanicals of much the same ilk as mine. Are you ill?'

Amazingly he coloured and looked away.

'No.'

A private worry, then, and one he did not wish to speak of? She had so often seen this reaction in patients and as surprising as it was in him she changed the subject completely.

'Would you be able to find the time to teach me how to ride properly, Lord Wesley?'

His eyes came back to hers, any hint of embarrassment gone. 'Why?'

'I dislike feeling…beaten by anything and you give the impression of knowing what you are doing around a horse.'

His frown deepened. 'Your uncle would allow it? My tuition, I mean.'

'Why should he not?'

'I have a certain reputation that generally worries the relatives of young débutantes.'

'I am not so young.'

He laughed. 'How old is "not young"?'

'Twenty-three.'

He laughed again. 'Believe me when I say that at my age your years look tender.'

'How old are you?'

'Thirty-four. A whole decade of experience ahead of yours.'

'Good.'

'Pardon?'

'I might need that if I am to cope here. Experience in handling others seems a requisite that is useful in the society salons of London.'

'Well, you managed Mr Friar on your own?'

She shook her head. 'No, it was the ill-placed plant holder at his feet that enabled me to vanquish him.'

'Luck is often as important as talent, Miss Ashfield, one learns that quickly.'

'Then I shall claim it was lucky that I met you, my lord; the one man in society with whom I seem to be able to have a reasonable conversation and who holds the same view upon marriage as I do.'

'Let me choose the horse, then.'

The twist in subject made her smile. He was good at putting people off guard. Unsure of what else to say, she nodded.

'Meet me in the park tomorrow at two. It won't be as busy as yesterday was at the later hour.'

'Very well. I shall pay you, of course, for the hire of the small and docile mount I have confidence you will choose for me and for your time.'

He smiled. 'How much?'

'I do not know exactly. What is the going rate?'

'More conversations just like this one, Miss Ashfield. And the chance to get to know you better.'

'Why would you want to?'

He smiled. 'You might be surprised if I answered that honestly.'

For just a moment something passed between them that Adelaide had never felt before, a breathless whirling knowledge of danger and desire. She stepped back, marvelling that, despite her shock, the implacable mask had not changed a whit on his handsome face.

'Perhaps, Lord Wesley, some time in your company may tarnish my desirability in the wifely stakes here. The spectacles do not quite seem to be accomplishing their given task.'

The round curse he used made her turn with

her armful of books and head back into the safety that the large numbers of men and women reading provided in the main room.

Damn it. Why did Gabriel Hughes have to be so beautiful? She would have liked it better if his face had been flawed and if she did not see the shadow of vulnerability that he hid so well beneath bravado and indifference. It was a friend she needed here, a confidant who was easy and biddable, one whom she could mould to any form she wanted. But the enigmatic Earl of Wesley was complex, difficult and unknowable, the small scar that ran beneath his ear on the right side only honing his beauty. He was… misleading. Yes, that was the word she wanted. Charm and danger both twisted together in a clever and menacing way. He was also interesting. Not wishing to dissect this thought for another second, she hurried to find her maid.

Miss Adelaide Ashfield was always running away, always scurrying in the other direction after sending him into a spin with some new and unexpected comment.

She wished to be tarnished? By him? Pain sliced through humour and regret chased hard on the heels of them both. He had not touched her but, oh, how he had wanted to, to feel the smooth softness of skin and the elegance of the line where her throat met the flesh sloping down to her breasts. He stopped still and closed his eyes. Waiting. Hoping. The whisper of her words, the fire in her eyes, her sharp tongue and the girlish romances buried amongst a weighty pile of scientific endeavour.

Contradictions.

Questions.

And nothing at all from his desiccated and useless member. Raising his left hand to his face, he breathed in deeply.

Lavender, arnica, comfrey and vinegar. A surprising combination. There were other things as well that he had no notion of.

'Hell,' he said to himself, Miss Adelaide Ashfield was the human embodiment of her salve. A healer. Brave. Unusual. Captivating. No wonder she had Lovelace and his ilk lapping at her heels.

He should cry off from the riding lessons, he

knew he should. If he had any goodness in him he would simply walk out of her life and let her get on with the task of being an innocent and unwilling débutante in London society. He had nothing to offer her, after all. More than nothing, he qualified, his body as burnt out as his custodial mansion.

Yet as one side of his mind dwelled upon the negative the other was already planning where and when he could organise their first riding lesson.

With irritation he felt the trembling he was now so often afflicted with. He didn't want her to know what a wreck he was, that was the problem, because in her eyes he saw reflected a version of himself that was still…honourable.

'Hell. Hell. Hell.'

With intent he moved the large map from above the botanical he had chosen on diseases of the body and settled down to peruse the index and look for his own particular malady and its stated cure.

Adelaide brushed out her hair before the mirror. What did Gabriel Hughes see when he saw her? she wondered. She was not beautiful in the way some other women here were, with their blond curls and alabaster skin. She was not dainty or feminine or curvy.

Brown. That was a word she might use to describe herself. Plain was another. She had not learned the art of flirting or dancing or conversing with a man as though everything he said was right and true and exact. Others here had that knack, she had watched them. The quiet flick of a fan and the twirling of an errant curl; the breathless looks that would reel a man in to produce the long sought-after offer of a hand in marriage.

Like a game. How often had Eloise or Jean told her of this and underlined the consequences marriage wrought on a woman's independence and pathway in life.

Kenneth Davis, the third-born son of Sir Nigel Davis, a squire on a neighbouring property, had then brought every warning to life. Adelaide shook her head, her eyes in the mirror darkening. She would try not to think of him.

It wasn't running away, she said to herself. No,

rather it was protecting her uncle and her cousin and the name of Penbury from a man who had clearly taken her offer of friendship and changed it into something that was different.

She hadn't told a soul other than her aunt Eloise about their exchange, either, preferring instead to sink back into the sanctuary of Northbridge and to the comforting other world of solitude. But sometimes at night when the moon was full and the land was covered in bright shadow she remembered.

She had been sixteen years old when she met Kenneth Davis behind the stables at midnight, creeping from her room with all the delight of one who expected compliments and perhaps a kiss. Small and trifling objects of his affection and regard.

The man who had met her was not the one she had known in the daytime, and when he had pulled at her gown and ripped it to her waist in one single dreadful movement, she was so frozen in shock that she could not even fight back.

Until his teeth bit at her nipples and his free hand seized the softer flesh beneath her skirt, his touch as unexpected and painful as the one at her breast. When she had tried to scream for help he had placed his hand across her mouth and pressed down hard.

'No more pretending, my sweetling. I have courted you for three whole months in all the small ways, but the real pleasure is here and now, in the dark.' His fingers came between her thighs, sharp and prodding, and the wine on his breath was strong as he swore.

He was drunk.

Drunk and dangerous and different.

In earnest she began to struggle, her knee coming up in the way Bertie had shown her, angled hard and direct to the groin. Kenneth Davis had fallen as if by magic, his mouth open, his breeches grotesquely arranged around his ankles so that the skin of his naked round bottom was pale in the moonlight.

Then she had run, with her tattered bodice, aching breasts and ruin, the stupidity of what she had allowed him beating against her reason. Tears could wait until she had once again gained the safety of her room and locked the door behind her.

Once there she had simply collapsed against the solidness of the wood, her legs like jelly as shock brought on a shaking and she had thoroughly gone to pieces.

She had made a mistake that was monumental and prodigious and far reaching in its consequences. Would Kenneth Davis tell anyone? Was she ravaged? Would she now have to marry a man she hated to the very last fibre of her being? What would her uncle say or her aunts?

This edge of horror was now the truth of her life as the scratches on her right breast throbbed in pain, burning as the night-time faded into dawn.

Aunt Eloise had found her in the morning, cold and stiff, and she had bathed her and dressed her and counselled silence.

'There is no way that you can win a war such as this one, Addie,' she had crooned as she pulled back the blankets and put her to bed. 'This is a truth women of all the ages have known.'

And so nothing had been said and life had regained its patterns and gone on.

In a different way for her, though. Fright filled the cracks of silence and Adelaide made certain that she was never far from her two old aunts. Nightmares replaced dreams, too, and for a good year afterwards she had barely slept.

Then Eloise and Jean had begun to teach her the art of healing, and in the elixirs and tinctures and ointments she had regained a peace long missing and a sense of herself that she had thought was lost.

Aye, in her reflection sometimes she still saw it, that terror and panic, but mostly now it was hidden under calm and manners, only a small ripple of a previous disquiet and seldom on show. Kenneth Davis himself had left summarily on an extended sojourn to Europe. She often wondered if his father had known something of his son's propensity for damage and drunkenness and had exiled him.

Almost eight years ago now, she whispered to herself. A day, a week, a month, a year. She had written down the passage of time as a list in her diaries, counting days and taking comfort from the distance and number as each year marched on. But she had never truly forgotten the horror and her uncle and cousin were the only men she allowed herself ever to be alone with.

But who was she now, she wondered, her eyes meeting the reflection in the silvered glass. Did a lack of trust hold one prisoner for ever, locked into celibacy and destined for spinsterhood?

'Please,' she whispered and then stopped. What was it she was asking for? The curl of hope turned inside darkness, like a frond of some fern in a deep and far-off forest. Nascent. Plump. Moving against shadow. Unfurling against Gabriel Hughes.

Because of his humour and kindness and beauty. His hands around her waist as he had helped her from the horse, his wariness in the library when she had asked him why he was reading a botanical, his lazy drawl as he had taken the pulse at George Friar's neck and commented on his appalling clothing.

She smiled. She would meet him again tomorrow in the park. At two. Her uncle had been surprisingly acquiescent. She had brought riding outfits down from Northbridge and, crossing the room, she opened the cupboard to bring them out across the bed.

Taking the shirt from one, she added it to the jacket of another. Finding a pin of bright red rubies, she placed it across the frothy collar. With her riding skirt this would look well upon her. She wondered if the hat she chose was not too…formal, but added it anyway as she had always liked the dark blue of the velvet.

Her fingers brushed up against the grain, the lush fabric a present from her uncle a year or so before. Her father's brother was a good man and he meant well. He would stay true to his word of allowing her home after the twelve weeks of Season, but just for a moment she wondered what might come to pass in the time left of her London stay. Gabriel Hughes's heartbreaking smile flashed into her memory.

Adelaide Ashfield's hands tightened on the leather reins with such a force that all her knuckles turned white.

'Fear looks like that, Miss Ashfield.' Gabriel pointed to the stiffness in her fingers. 'Demeter will know you tremble through the leather and it'll worry her.' Reaching up, he released the reins. 'Just grip like this and let the leather run over the top. See? Then cup them so that there is space to move.'

'She won't pull away?'

'Try it.'

'Now?'

'I am here beside you. Walk around the pathway and if she becomes fidgety I will stop her.'

She nodded, though Gabriel could see her composure was taking some effort.

'After the other day, riding a horse does not feel as safe as it should.'

'The steed you nearly fell from was largely untrained. Does your uncle have no idea of an animal's temperament or of your ability to manage one?'

'Well, he rides sometimes, but, no, I suppose there is not much need for expertise at Northbridge because we seldom venture out further than the village.'

As the mount began to move she took in a hard breath.

'This isn't the small and docile steed I had imagined you might pick for me, Lord Wesley. Did you get her at Coles?'

'No, she's mine.'

'Oh. No wonder she is so beautiful, then.'

He began to laugh. 'You think I only keep attractive horses in my stable?'

'Well, rumour has it you are a man of good taste…in whatever you try.'

'The titter-tattle of the *ton* in play, no doubt. Wait till you hear what else is said of me. Ahh, but I can see from your face that you have. Bear it in mind that my reputation is one magnified by the interest in it and if I had slept with every woman I am said to have I'd have barely been out of bed. These days I am far more circumspect.'

She looked at him directly then, censure in the water-marked blue. 'Brothels are not more circumspect, my lord, in anyone's language.'

A thread of irritation surfaced. 'The tongues of those with little to recommend them save gossip are seldom still. If you could take it on yourself to disbelieve at least half of what is said of me, the picture might be a truer one.'

'An angel, then? The personification of your name?' Her irony was harsh.

'Hardly that. Were I to proffer an excuse at all it would probably be a lack of paternal guidance. My father was a violent drunk.'

'Well, at least you had one. Mine was killed when I was not yet four years old.'

'*Touché*, Miss Ashfield. Has anyone ever told you that you are beautiful when you are angry?'

The wash of red caught him by surprise. Her blush was intense and unsettling and wide eyes stood out amidst it.

'No, of course not. And they would be lying if they did. I am not beautiful, Lord Wesley, not in the way the *ton* defines beauty and I have no wish to be. Passable is all that I aim for. And interesting,' she added, her top teeth worrying her bottom lip after she had said it.

Despite meaning not to his hand reached out for the arm nearest to him and he laid his fingers across hers. 'If you think I was lying, then you have no knowledge of me at all, Miss Ashfield.'

The park around them dissolved into empty space and without warning a feeling that Gabriel had long since thought dead, rose. It was so unexpected that the world disappeared into whiteness, the dizzying bout of relief making him sway, an unusual heat creeping into the very bones of emotion and wringing out the bitterness.

'God.' The breath was knocked out of his body in shock and confusion.

Adelaide Ashfield was off her horse in a second, a dismount that was as rapid and competent as any he had ever seen.

'Are you well, Lord Wesley?'

He held his fists so tightly curled that they hurt.

'I…am.' Fighting to get the words out, he closed his eyes. Not panic now, but sheer and utter relief. If he could feel like this once, then it stood to reason he could do so again. He swallowed back a thickness and took in air, reaching for the return of that he had imagined never to know again.

'If you describe your symptoms to me, I am more than certain I could find something to help you?'

The laughter in his throat warred with a heady disbelief and that in turn was swallowed by a certain and horrifying realisation.

She had no idea what she was doing to him, this unusual and tall country miss with her ocean-blue eyes and honesty. Already she was digging into the pocket of her skirt to bring forth a twist of powder that was the colour of mud.

'I had this on hand for myself, my lord. Light-headedness comes from fear, you see, and I imagined I may have had need for it. But you...?'

He shook his head, not wishing for any medicine that might eliminate the effect of warm blood on his masculinity. 'Perhaps we might... postpone this riding...lesson, then, until another day...Miss Ashfield.' Sweat had begun to build above his top lip and temples.

'You are too overheated?' Her face looked aghast.

'Just...breathless.' Each word took effort, and, gesturing to the maid who sat on a bench twenty feet from them, he moved back, the reins of his horses in his hands held as tightly as he had been instructing her not to.

And then he was off his horse, walking, striding towards the park gate and glad that the pathway out of the gardens was clear.

Once through them, he stopped. What the hell had just happened? He wanted to go back and try again, take her hand and see if perhaps the feeling might grow and blossom into the hope of more. A proper erection. The return of his libido. But he couldn't. Cowardice had a certain all-consuming feel to it and if it was an illusion, then…? He shook his head and mounted his horse for home.

Adelaide watched him go, her brow knitted in worry. She hadn't a clue as to what was wrong with Lord Wesley, but the colour had flooded from his face as if sudden pain had consumed him and he had swayed so markedly she had thought he would faint.

If Aunt Eloise and Aunt Jean were here they would have probably known his troubles exactly, but they were long gone.

Milly stood watching him, too, puzzlement on her face. 'Perhaps his lordship is still hurt from the incident with the horse in the park the other day, ma'am, and is not telling us.'

Or he is truly sick, she thought, her worry growing. The botanical she had seen him reading in Lackington's was a sign of something not being right and his symptoms here underlined that fact.

She had enough experience to also know some men loathed discussing any ailment they suffered with a woman, and the knowledge that she was not a trained healer would be a further deterrent. Still, a small sense of sorrow stirred in such a lack of trust.

'Say nothing of this to my uncle, Milly. I am certain once the earl is feeling better we can continue the lessons.'

Chapter Seven

Once home Gabriel helped himself to a stiff brandy and sat down to mull over his afternoon.

He had felt something there in the parts of him that had been numb and dead for a full six months. He could barely believe it. Was he cured? Was this the beginning of a healing he had been so certain was beyond hope?

It had begun the moment he had laid his fingers down across hers and felt an answering tug that had been soft and gentle. Unexpected. Impossibly real. Not the full-blown nakedness of practised courtesans or the come-hither sexual play of a country whore. Just a gentle quiet gesture in the middle of a busy park.

He closed his eyes and breathed in hard.

How was that even possible?

A knock on the door had him standing as his butler announced there was a visitor. Not just any visitor, either, but Mrs Cressida Murray and newly returned from the north. Cressie and he had once been lovers before she had left for Yorkshire and a marriage with a local landowner of some note.

Her face, as she came into the room, was as beautiful as he remembered it to be, though her eyes were somewhat reddened. 'I am sorry to bother you, Wesley, but I had no one else that I could turn to and I need help.'

She removed her coat when he failed to reply and her breasts almost sprang from the very low neckline of a deep red day dress. Then she flung herself into his arms and kissed him full on the lips.

Nothing. He felt nothing. His stomach did not turn with the sickness and his heart failed to pound with the closeness. A new development, this. A further difference in the reactions of his body. Today was one of such constant surprise he could barely keep up.

'It is so very good to see you again, Gabriel.'

Smiling through unease, he extricated himself from her grasp and turned to pour them both a drink. The strong brandy made him feel less edgy.

With the intimacy of Cressida Murray's kiss, and after his encounter with Adelaide Ashfield, he might have expected some warming, but there had been none. Another problem. A further disquiet? One moment hot and the next cold and no middle ground where compromise could result in a cure? Shaking away the thought, he made himself concentrate on what his unexpected visitor was saying.

'I have come because I need a partner for the Whitely ball and I want him to be you.'

'Why?'

'My husband has cheated on me and I have reached the conclusion that if he wants to play at this game then he needs to know I can, too.' Her voice wobbled as she went on. 'I think he needs to know that I am a beautiful woman whom he is lucky to be married to, a woman whom he should not leave alone up in the wilds of Yorkshire whilst he cavorts with others here.'

There was something in her voice that held Gabriel's attention, some quiet and vulnerable honesty. After his shock today he was more in tune with the nuances in others. He waited as she went on.

'I love him. For his good points and his bad, but this…dalliance in London needs to stop. He needs to come home to Yorkshire and give our marriage a chance again.'

Without warning Cressida went to pieces, her tears and sobs filling the room. With trepidation Gabriel moved forward to hold her, till the storm had passed and she had quietened, pleased again when her closeness did not seem to affect him in the slightest. After a good few moments she looked up at him through tear-filled eyes.

'You were always the sort of man that women truly liked, Gabriel, and not only for the way you look. Gavin and I are…having problems and I could not think of anyone else to come to for help without it being all over town come the morning. I need a companion who is attentive and well regarded by the ladies. One who might make my husband jealous without expecting anything in return.'

'So you want me to…?' He stopped, leaving the question in the air.

'Flirt with me at the Whitely ball and dance at least twice with me.'

He began to laugh. 'And will I be called out at dawn by this husband of yours because of it?'

'Oh, if he did do that it would be wonderful, but I wouldn't like you to shoot him or anything.'

Gabriel had to smile at her convoluted reasoning. 'He's a big man, if I recall…'

'But clumsy with it.'

'And he has numerous brothers?'

She nodded. 'Four, but I cannot envisage him ever hurting a soul. Please, Gabriel. You owe me this one favour at least.'

'I do?' He tried to think of why.

'You left me with barely a word. That hurt. A lot. And the one promise you did make before you disappeared was that you were sorry and that if there was anything you could do to make things easier…' She stopped. 'This is the thing you can do to make it easier. I am calling in the favour.'

'I see.'

'Do you? You broke my heart once and Gavin put it back together again. You have no idea of your effect on women and you have never once really been so much in love that you care.'

Her words cut into the quick of truth. Henrietta Clements had said almost the same thing to him and the guilt stung. He couldn't ever make it up to her, but here with Cressida he had the chance of redemption.

'God. I can think of a hundred reasons why this scheme of yours will not work.'

Warm fingers came into the cold of his palm. 'But you will try?'

Adelaide and her uncle and chaperon arrived a lot later at the Whitely ball than they had intended to, Lady Harcourt's brother having visited in the afternoon and staying on until well after dinner.

The theme of the soirée was an underwater one with long strands of shiny green silk hanging from the ceiling around all the four walls of the room. With the lighting dimmed and the chandeliers painted blue the whole place appeared almost unreal. Huge statues of sea gods graced the room; Neptune seated in a shell pulled by seahorses, the goddesses behind with the Tritons and other various nymphs. Fish sculpted from blocks of ice sat on the many scattered tables.

Adelaide had never seen anything remotely like this excess before and even Imelda was speechless as they walked through into the throngs of people.

'Lady Whitely has quite outdone herself this year, I think. Rumour has it that it might be their last big party so we are so lucky to be a part of it. Something to remember with a thrill, I think, my dear. I know I shall.'

The crush tonight was far more noticeable than it had been all Season and it was hard to even move from one side of the room to the other.

'Should you not miss this sort of excitement if you do decide to return to Northbridge, Adelaide?'

Her uncle asked the question, his interest in her answer obvious.

'Indeed, there is something to be said of the scope and wonder of the London soirées. But perhaps after a while a certain indifference might set in.'

Alec laughed and gestured to a passing footman to bring them each a drink.

Adelaide looked around to see whether the Earl of Wesley was in attendance, but she could not see him at all. The room was a large one, but partitions divided it into two and she wondered if he could be further down towards a band she could hear playing. Standing on her toes, she tried to see if she could find him.

'Who are you looking for?' Imelda Harcourt raised her lorgnette. 'Ahhh, there is Berrick, my dear, and he does look well tonight. Why, I do believe he is coming our way. Smile, Adelaide. Men like to see a welcoming face, not a dour one, and you look so much prettier when you are happy.'

If Eloise or Jean could have heard such advice they would have been far from pleasant, but the guileless and earnest way her chaperon expressed such a sentiment made Adelaide smile. Lady Harcourt honestly believed that she was helping, that a woman's role was as an adjunct to a well-connected and wealthy man and that a good marriage made the whole world right.

This was the way of London society. A way to survive and prosper and never let those from the strata below gain a foot up in the world. Solidarity and isolation buoyed by the cohesiveness of the *ton*.

As the Earl of Berrick joined them Adelaide took in breath and made a conscious effort to be at least polite.

She did not see Lord Wesley until almost halfway through the night and any joy that she had from noticing him was snatched away by the beautiful girl beside him, his hand resting lightly on the sway of her back.

She was like a porcelain doll, with blond hair arranged into a cascade of curls, brown eyes that sparkled even from this distance and a dress that mirrored the theme of the evening. Blue-green shots of silk radiated around her and Adelaide gained the impression of a sea creature long hidden and suddenly revealed in exactly the setting she should be.

A large crowd had gathered about them and when the woman's hand crept into the crook of Gabriel Hughes's arm, he laid his own across it in return.

They were so perfectly matched Adelaide could not look away though her heart was thumping in a fashion that she did not like. Almost scared, she thought. Of what?

'Mrs Gavin Murray is back, I see.' Even Imelda for all her short-sightedness had noticed the couple. 'I knew her mother once and what a time she had with that girl, I can tell you.'

'She is very beautiful.'

Imelda nodded. 'Yes, that she is and strong willed with it. It seems the marriage to her Yorkshire beau has come to nothing, then, and she has her talons into the Earl of Wesley once more.'

Her uncle then asked the question Adelaide wanted to.

'Once more?'

'They were an item a few years back and all thought the banns would be called and the deed done. But Lord Wesley went off to the Continent and she disappeared up north and the next thing we knew she had tied the knot with a Mr Gavin Murray. No connection to the Murrays of the *ton*, either, but rich in their own right. Her mother was not pleased, but in the light of the Wesley family fire and its failing fortunes perhaps Cressida made a wise choice…then.'

'The Wesleys had a fire?' Adelaide did not wait for her uncle to ask a further question.

'The family manor of Ravenshill was damaged badly six or so months back and if gossip is to be believed they have not the wherewithal to have it rebuilt. It is why Lord Wesley is here, I suppose. He has finally been brought to the heel of Holy Matrimony by the dire circumstances of an expected financial ruin. Cressida Murray is, however, a poor choice given every other wealthy and unattached woman in the room would probably take him in an instant. Beauty has a certain allure, you understand, but I doubt even with a ring on his finger Gabriel Hughes would have the wherewithal to be faithful.'

Suddenly collecting herself, Imelda Harcourt snapped open her fan. 'His grandfather, Lytton Hughes, was just the same. Every judicious and level-headed girl in court was made half-witted by him and it is happening again. Here.'

A slight stammer led Adelaide to believe the older Hughes patriarch had been important to Imelda somehow.

'The Wesley men are like well-formed rainbows, capturing everyone's notice, but disappearing at the first sign of permanence. Mark my words, Lord Wesley will take what is on offer and then he will leave.'

When Adelaide looked over towards the couple it certainly did seem as though the earl was enjoying himself. He was leading Cressida Murray into a dance now, a waltz, and when he pulled her into his arms there was no space left between them.

Looking away, she was angry with herself for this close observation. Of course a man like Gabriel Hughes would choose a woman of the same ilk: magnificent, resplendent and striking.

Lucy Carrigan chose that moment to come forward and speak and when she saw where Adelaide had been gazing she shook her head.

'They have been the talk of the ball all night

because the Earl of Wesley has hardly been a foot from her side. Her husband has just arrived, too, if you can believe it, and yet still she has no shame.'

'Husband. My God.' Adelaide glanced around in consternation. Even given the dubious standards of behaviour amongst the very wealthy of the *ton* she could not imagine this to be…acceptable. 'Where is he?'

'The dark-haired man over there by the pillar with a face of thunder.'

'The man standing in the company of two others all of the same build and colouring?'

Lucy nodded. 'His brothers, and they do not look remotely happy.'

The crush seemed to be the only thing that was saving a skirmish, a hundred bodies between adversaries and a good few moments of pushing.

As Adelaide took in a breath the golden glance of Lord Wesley fell directly upon her before sliding away. No recognition or humour was apparent in his hard and glittering observation. In fact, he looked furious.

* * *

Damn it. Adelaide Ashfield was here. Watching him like half of the *ton* was with bated breath and undeniable interest. He had hoped against hope that Adelaide might not have attended to-night but been elsewhere instead.

It was not every day, after all, that a love triangle was played out in such an obvious public space. God, if he had been them he'd probably be looking, too. But for a second the smile on his face faltered. He didn't want Adelaide here watching this and there was no way now he could insist on it being any different.

'My husband is coming over, Gabe.' Cressida whispered this into his ear. 'Remember that no matter what happens you promised me you would not hurt him.'

The stakes rose again, an assurance of non-action balanced against the safety of those around them and weighed out in the presence of Murray and his two brothers. Nay, three, he amended as the third burly Murray joined the group.

If he had any sense he would leave now, simply turn and make his way out of the room with his tail between his legs and his face intact.

But other things also mattered. His honour. His troth to Cressida and the ignominy that such a cowardly retreat might paint in the eyes of Miss Adelaide Ashfield.

Around them space had opened, an amazing feat in itself given the numbers in the room. A footman dressed as a sea sprite and carrying a well-stocked tray tottered through the emptiness with no inkling of the tension. Gabriel pushed down the need for a drink. If he was to have his teeth knocked out by the jealous fit of a furious husband, he did not want to be holding crystal.

'Gavin.' Cressida's voice was breathless as her unhappy spouse came to a halt in front of them, her hand dropping from Gabriel's arm.

'I have come to take you home.' Murray's tone was anything but friendly.

'To Yorkshire?' Gabriel could hear the hope in Cressida's words, but the dolt of a man seemed to miss it altogether, simply striding forward and laying a heavy blow to his right eye.

At any other time Gabriel would have fought

back with ease. He prayed that the brothers might get involved because he hadn't made a troth concerning them and was itching to beat someone up as the full force of pain kicked in.

The second blow was delivered to his mouth and he could taste blood as he went down, the third landing squarely on his temple and blackening his vision.

Cressida, to give her some credit, leant towards him and whispered, 'I am so sorry, Gabriel. If you stay still, he is not a man to kick someone when they are vanquished.' But Gabriel could not have moved if he had tried, the breath gone from him. As she turned to join her husband, Gavin Murray did away with any last shred of humanity and lashed out with his boot, connecting heavily with the soft tissue of Gabriel's back.

Then they left, heads held high as they threaded through the crowd, Cressida tucked within them like a diminutive and valued prize that the Murrays had come to collect.

The green light and the sea creatures swam before him in a dizzying blur, the pain of the blows setting in and making him shake. Then there was a hand on his brow and the soft words of Miss Adelaide Ashfield in his ear.

'You should have fought back, Lord Wesley. There was no reason for you not to.'

Gabriel swallowed and then spat. Blood dripped from his nose and his mouth, the sour tang of copper out of place here amongst luxury and excess.

'Don't stay here, Adelaide. It is too dangerous for you.'

Already he could hear the whispers all around and the hem of her skirt was splattered with red.

'But you are hurt and I can help.'

He shook his head. 'If you stand and leave now, your reputation may not quite be ruined. Please.'

He watched the worry in her eyes turn into anger.

And then she was gone, the blue of her gown disappearing between the legs and skirts of all those within his vision, the floor slippery with his own blood as he sat up, trying not to look at anyone.

Alone.

This is what his life had felt like for so very

long. The fury within him vibrated as he made himself stand and walk from the room.

'Why would you even think to interfere, Adelaide? You must have realised what a scandal Wesley had caused and how fitting his punishment was. And now you have placed yourself at risk and at peril, an accessory to the fact of marital disharmony and your dress ruined.'

Her uncle was furious, though Imelda stayed very quiet on the other side of the carriage, her fingers tightly wrapped around the stem of an ancient silver cane.

'Why on earth did you try to help him? You, a débutante, a young woman, a girl of grace and tender years? What possible thought could have been going through your head to imagine you should be the one to do this?'

'No one else was, Uncle.'

Alec laughed at that, but the sound wasn't kind. 'Perhaps, after all, you should not have come to London. Perhaps I should have allowed you to stay at Sherborne and live the sort of life your aunts favoured because now…' he faltered '…because now I do not know what to do.'

Imelda chose that moment to add her twopenn'orth.

'We can wait to see how the land lies in the morning, Penbury. Adelaide's foolish reaction may after all be attributed to a kind heart or an innocent foolishness. There may be some dividend in that.'

'Dividend? Did you see the other girls rush forward? No. They were far too sensible to get themselves embroiled in such a scandal. Lord Wesley is trouble with his wild ways and insolence and good common sense has taught them to keep well clear of a man who ruins everything he touches.'

'He was not the one throwing the punches, Uncle.'

'Because he knew he was in the wrong. God binds a man and a woman together for eternity in marriage and only a dissolute womaniser would want to interfere with that.'

Her uncle looked out the window after this outburst and Adelaide did the same. The lights of London flickered by in myriad colours, the streets almost empty of people as bells somewhere rang out the late hour of two. In the reflection of the glass she could see the stilled outline of Alec and the smaller form of Lady Harcourt. Her own face, too, was mirrored back, her hair tied in an intricate form that had taken her maid, Milly, an hour to secure.

For nothing. For disaster. She wondered what had happened after they had left. Had anyone helped Gabriel Hughes or had he limped off out of the mêlée with a curse? Or not left at all? Had worse things happened? Had the Murrays waited outside for him and beaten him again? Was he now lying somewhere no one could find him? She shook her head against such worries.

The Earl of Wesley had barely looked at her and he had been furious. He'd made no effort at all to protect himself, either in words or in actions, though she knew without any shadow of a doubt that he was nowhere near as civilised as he seemed. Why had he not fought back? Why had he allowed the husband of a woman he must have expected to confront him beat the daylights out of his non-resistance and so very publically? Nothing of it made any sense.

'Lord Berrick will probably withdraw his interest in courting you now.' Her uncle's words broke into the silence. 'And although your fortune is substantial, Adelaide, every family of the *ton* would shy away from a girl who shows such poor judgement in a social situation.'

'I see.'

'No, you don't, my dear.' A thread of cynicism that was unusual for Alec Ashfield could be heard in his words. 'With just a little good sense you could have made a glorious union and now…now they will all be fleeing and you will be left, unattached, unwanted and ill thought of. There is sadness in that which will become more poignant as you age and miss out on all the milestones of your counterparts.'

Adelaide frowned. In his words were the seeds of truth, she thought. Lady Imelda simply stared at her and said nothing.

Cressida Murray sent a note to his town house the next morning, the flourish of ink enquiring after his health and telling him that she would be leaving that day with her husband to go back to Yorkshire and that he was not to contact her again.

Gabriel screwed the paper up and threw it into the fire where the dainty sheet of paper was caught in orange flame and disappeared.

No doubt Gavin Murray had been present when she had written it, but he was glad for the closure. He now owed her nothing. A debt paid in full.

Crossing the room, he looked into the mirror and almost smiled at the face that stared back at him. Hardly recognisable, his left eye swollen closed and his lip split. But it was the bruise that spread from ear to cheek that was the most noticeable, a broken blood vessel that had marked and darkened the surrounding tissue.

Nothing that could not heal though, he thought, as he took Adelaide Ashfield's lavender concoction down from the shelf and layered it thickly over the places that hurt. The ointment had worked like magic on his knuckles and had eased some of the scarring on his thigh. He hoped it would do the same for his face.

He imagined the gossip that must be swirling around the *ton* this morning after the spectacle last night. God, if he did not have his mother to look after and Ravenshill Manor to rebuild he'd be off on the next sailing to the Americas. Somewhere far and wild and free. Somewhere he could make his own way in a world not bound by propriety and manners and expectations.

A knock on the door had him looking up and Daniel Wylde and Lucien Howard both entered the room.

'Hope you don't mind the intrusion, Gabe. We heard about the altercation last night and came to see if you were still alive.'

'Just.'

The three of them smiled.

'From all accounts you simply allowed Murray to beat the daylights out of you?' The words were phrased as a question and as Gabriel pulled down three glasses and filled them with his best brandy, he nodded.

'I'd given my promise not to retaliate.'

'To Cressida Murray?'

'She loves her husband. I was caught up in the ruse of it.'

'Why?'

'I owed her—'

'Not that much, surely,' Lucien interrupted. 'And what the hell is on your face?'

'A lavender ointment Miss Ashfield made up for me.'

'Miss Adelaide Ashfield from Sherborne? The Penbury niece?'

'The same.'

'I hear she was the only one who tried to help you last night. Her reputation has fallen a little because of it. Seems as if she could well be packed off back to the country by her uncle, ruined by her ill-thought-out kindness.'

'Who told you that?'

'My mother over breakfast.' Lucien's words were quiet.

Daniel Wylde had the temerity to laugh. 'And the countess is always so well informed. Personally, I think Adelaide Ashfield's star may have risen for such actions prove only compassion and tender-heartedness. And bravery. On that score my wife would like for you to come to dinner tomorrow night, Gabriel. At the town house. She has told me that she will not brook a refusal and is down in London only for the week.'

'I am certain the *ton* would frown at her invite if they knew of it.'

'That's why she wants you to come. Amethyst seldom graces any society function. She is of the opinion that anyone who so flagrantly breaks the strict code of manners needs to be encouraged and expects you at eight. Luce is coming, and Francis. He is off to the Americas in a week or so, after the hope of gold and a clue he said you had given him.'

'The chancy pot at the end of a rainbow?'

'Not to St Cartmail.' Lucien's laughter was loud.

'You had better enlighten him, then, Gabe. For if he dies in his quest for gold his demise will be squarely on your head.' Daniel's interjection was measured.

'And if he discovers riches, will it be the same?' Gabriel finished his drink and placed the glass down half-on and half-off the edge of the mahogany table, teetering between safety and peril. 'There is risk in everything. Take that away and life goes, too.'

'The philosophy of jeopardy? Stated like a man with nothing to lose.' Lucien sounded like he was out of patience and Daniel took over.

'Come tomorrow night at eight, then. Bring a bottle or two of this brandy.'

'I doubt Amethyst would want to gaze at my face in this condition. It would probably put her off her food.'

'Nothing much could do that at the moment, Gabe. She is heavily pregnant with our second child and starving.'

'And you have only been married a little under two years.'

'Amethyst wants our brood to meet their grandfather before he dies. If Robert lives for ever, which he looks likely to do despite his heart condition, we will be overrun with progeny. Not that I am complaining.'

And he wasn't, Gabriel thought. Daniel Wylde was a man with a family and a place and a wife who was unusual and interesting. He had not stuck to the rules of the *ton*, but lived outside of them well and happily.

Perhaps he could do the same?

'Could an invite be sent to Miss Adelaide Ashfield as well? I should like to apologise to her for the problems that I have caused her and I doubt the Viscount of Penbury will allow me anywhere near the house now.'

'It can.' In the two words Gabriel heard both humour and question, but he chose to ignore it.

Chapter Eight

An invitation arrived for Adelaide just after lunch, the Wyldes' servant waiting at the front door for an answer.

'The Earl of Montcliffe and his wife have invited you for dinner tomorrow night?' Her uncle was incredulous. 'Have they not heard of the problems at the Whitely ball?'

Imelda broke in. 'Daniel Wylde and his new wife seldom come to anything in London. I hear they spend most of their time in the family seat outside of Barnet, but they are respectable and well thought of. Lady Montcliffe is from trade, of course, though extremely rich in her own right. As I have not heard a bad word about them perhaps we should view this as a chance of…reinstating your niece's reputation in society.'

'She'd need to be chaperoned.'

'Bertram could accompany her. He is an acquaintance of Wylde, after all, and it is well past time to allow him some familial responsibility.'

Adelaide's heart beat faster. Lord Montcliffe was also a friend of Lord Wesley. Had Gabriel Hughes been invited, too? Without Imelda Harcourt there and with her cousin in tow she might be given a greater amount of freedom to speak with him. She waited to see what her uncle might say.

'Very well. As you so rightly argue, Imelda, this might be a way to restore yourself, Adelaide. Pray this time you will remember all your manners and responsibilities to our family name. I will instruct Bertram to return you home by twelve.'

'Thank you, Uncle.' She tried to keep gratitude from her voice and made an effort to avert her eyes lest Alec see the spark of excitement that she knew would be within them and change his mind completely.

Gabriel followed Daniel Wylde as he ushered him into a salon at the front of the house. It was a familiar room. Once a good few years back this had been like a second home to him but then Daniel had been called off to the Peninsular War and Gabriel had met Henrietta.

Amethyst Wylde stood to greet him as he came into the chamber. On the few occasions he had met her Gabriel had found her to be a woman of wit and cleverness who seemed to have little time for the inconsequential chatter and precise manners of the *ton*.

'Lord Wesley, it is good to see you again.' As her eyes ran over his face she did not look away. Rather she observed each injury closely. 'Christine Howard is adamant Gavin Murray is a bully and a cheat. She also swears that his wife would have been much better off under your protection.'

Gabriel smiled. 'I beg to disagree, my lady. Beating him into a pulp would not have solved a thing.'

'So you allowed him to beat you into a pulp instead?'

The anger expressed on his behalf was surprising and he smiled. 'Perhaps I did.'

'Well, then, let us just pray that your sacrifice

might count for something. A man who kicks
another whilst down and out must have his own
set of dubious morals. An uneasy and dangerous fault to live with, I should imagine, for Mrs
Cressida Murray.'

Gabriel had the feeling Daniel Wylde was listening carefully, though the way he looked at his
wife and took her hand had him glancing away.
Solidarity and unity had a certain heat to it. A
conversation from an adjoining room suddenly
caught his attention.

'Lucien and Francis are here, too, Gabriel as
well as Miss Ashfield and her cousin Bertram
Ashfield. There will be seven of us altogether
because Lucien has brought his sister, Christine.'

Adelaide was in the next salon? So she had
come? Sweeping back the length of his unruly
hair, Gabriel followed his hosts through the open
doors.

She was sitting on the sofa when he saw her,
but she stood almost immediately, wide blue eyes
through glass taking in the bruising on his cheek
in that particular way she had of noticing things.

'Miss Ashfield.'

'Lord Wesley.' Stiff and uncertain. He was careful not to reach out for her hand or make any effort to touch her in such a public domain.

'I hope you thought to use my ointment on your face, my lord?'

Before he could answer Bertram Ashfield spoke. 'Addie is a wizard at the art of healing. Our old and unmarried aunts were the same and she has followed their example.'

Addie. Gabriel turned the name on his tongue— a family nickname that suited her entirely. But her cousin was not yet finished.

'At Sherborne, Adelaide has a clinic that is always full of those interested in her concoctions. I think she could make a fortune if she were to set up a business for the dispensing of medicines.'

'Well, we could certainly do with that.' Francis's interjection made Lucien laugh. When Adelaide looked puzzled, Francis St Cartmail continued on to explain.

'We call ourselves "The Penniless Lords", Miss Ashfield. A half joke at our expense, I know, although Daniel has seen fit to remedy his desperate circumstances and in the nicest way possible.'

Amethyst Wylde took up the cause. 'If I had sisters, I should send them straight into your direction, Francis.' Her eyes alighted on Adelaide. 'You have a fortune, do you not, Miss Ashfield? Perhaps one of these lords might catch your eye?'

Unbelievably Adelaide blushed a bright red, though Amethyst quickly spoke again as if to take attention from her. 'I have a garden at Montcliffe you might be interested in. It has a large variety of different herbs and flowers and you would be most welcome to gather any specimens that caught your fancy. I know if one is passionate about a subject one is always on the lookout for new and different material. My papa is like that. Timber is his love and he can seldom pass a mill without going in to see what is on offer. Daniel's is horses.'

Bertram Ashfield was quick to catch on to the new subject and after a moment the group split and Gabriel stood alone with Adelaide.

'I am glad to see you here, my lord. I expected at least some broken bones.'

'Oh, I have a knack at fending off blows, Miss Ashfield, and surviving them.'

'I have heard it mentioned that you were a champion at the sport of sparring'

'That was some while ago. I have not pursued the activity for years.'

'Still, it must be like horse riding. Once learned, never forgotten.'

He smiled. 'What is it you are trying to say, Adelaide?'

The use of her Christian name seemed to take her by surprise because the same flush from before spread across her cheeks.

'I want to know why you didn't retaliate against Mr Murray in the crowded ballroom?'

'Because I had made a promise not to.'

'A promise to his wife?'

He smiled at her quickness. 'Cressida Murray's husband had been caught cheating. She wanted to encourage him back.'

'By sleeping with you?'

No other woman of his acquaintance would have voiced such a question, but there was something in Adelaide Ashfield that was different. 'Hardly. It was jealousy she was after.'

Blue eyes blazed. 'Asking for such an impossible favour implies more than a passing friendship between you, my lord.'

He looked her directly. 'I hurt her once, badly. Perhaps I deserved it.'

A small frown played about her brow. 'One cannot always be responsible for the feelings of others, sir. Revenge lies in one's own hands, I would hope, and not in the battered face of a former lover caught under an unreasonable promise.'

'You think penance is unreasonable, then, in the repayment of a debt?'

'Her penance or yours?'

Hell. Could mind reading be another of Miss Ashfield's unusual gifts? His temple ached, the burr of voices making it worse, and to top it all off he had the deep-felt impression that she was enjoying this.

Taking stock of his irritation, he changed the topic. 'I have heard that you suffered for your kindness to me at the Whitely ball and I am sorry for it.'

'Well, the Earl of Berrick and the Honourable Richard Williams have turned tail and run. I would not call that suffering. Perhaps it should be me who is thanking you.'

Startled by her honesty, Gabriel laughed. He could barely remember the last time he had done so out of her company.

'You have a fortune, Miss Ashfield. There will be a great number of willing swains behind that lot and of a far better calibre if you just give it time.'

'I hope not. Uncle Alec seems to think my unseemly behaviour at the ball was unforgivable. He is considering packing me off to Sherborne again to live out my days in Dorset in a spinsterly regret.'

'And will you?'

'Regret my lack of a marriage proposal?' She swallowed and Gabriel wondered if she was quite as impervious to her suitors as she made out. Lord, if she was carted off back to Sherborne he'd lose the chance of talking to her again and feeling…something? He dared not risk touching her here, but he wanted to. The ache of desire to discern his body's reaction to her almost undid him.

Her hand lay on the headrest of the chair she stood by, the nails short and tidy, her fingers dainty. A healer's hand. He could see the blue veins through the thin whiteness of her skin. There was a burn on one of her knuckles and it had blistered. From assembling her concoctions, perhaps? He hoped it had not happened when she had made the lavender ointment for him.

A great wave of melancholy kept him rooted to the spot, the emptiness of his life leaving a stillness that was unending. Usually he found some relief in humour, but tonight he could not seem to do that, the truth of all that he wasn't, shocking.

If he were to touch her and feel only indifference, then that was the end of it for him. Excusing himself, he moved away with barely the minimum of manners.

Lucien found him over by the small cabinet that held Daniel's fine brandy. 'You look exhausted, Gabe. Perhaps a holiday in the country at your family seat is in order?'

'Amongst the smouldering ashes of Ravenshill

Manor and its roofless walls?' Gabriel returned and Lucien Howard began to laugh wryly.

'I had forgotten about the fire. What the hell happened between us a few years back, Gabe? Why did you just disappear without word or reason? Daniel and I tried to find you before we left for Spain, but you were gone.'

Gone into hell, Gabriel thought, and took a drink, lost in the clutches of Henrietta Clements and the political intrigues of her husband.

What was it Gracian had said in his treatise on worldly wisdom? *'Never open the door to a lesser evil, for other greater ones invariably slink on in.'* One mistake leads to the next and the next until there is no way left to go.

That was how he had felt, still felt even six months after the fire. Once, he might have managed, but now…only guilt was left and a floundering pool of regret.

What had Daniel and Cressida both said of him? That he was kind. The lie of that made his stomach feel hollow; he was his father's son, a man full of anger and retribution.

The truth of it scalded against honour as he upended the brandy.

* * *

Adelaide wished she could just go home away from this house and these people and the gaiety of a salon filled with friends. Close friends—a group who were relaxed in each other's company and at ease with the expressing of strong opinion. The Earl of Wesley patently was barely interested in her appearance here.

Her cheeks still scalded her from the earlier blush and she chastised herself. But it was hard to appear as indifferent as she would have liked to when he was standing a few feet away from her with his beautiful face so bruised and broken.

He seemed more reticent tonight, less relaxed, the muscles of his jawbone grinding in a constant motion. She had glanced across at him a moment or so before and caught him watching her, the pale gold gaze pulled away as soon as their eyes met. He was drinking a lot, too.

Tormented. The word came from nowhere, but sat across explanation with a quietly formed ease. If the demons in him were circling even here amongst friends in a cosy London town house, then imagine what they must do at other more lonely times.

Heartsick or soul sick, she wondered, looking at the pulse in his throat. Faster than it should be at rest and his hand trembled as he reached for the brandy bottle. Perhaps he had loved Cressida Murray and was drowning in the sorrow of her betrayal— -a wretched public denouncement at that, the bruises on him testament to a sense of honour that was startling.

He'd kept his word. He had not hit back. From the way he looked Adelaide doubted such decency was much of a consolation to him. Indeed, he gave the singular impression that he would like to fling his fist through the hard wall behind him and keep bashing until pain scoured wrath and sanity returned.

She had seen the look Lucien Howard had given Daniel Wylde when he'd joined them at the drinks cabinet.

Be careful, he's suffering and I don't know how the hell to change it.

Adelaide had always been good at reading the nuances, postures and expressions of others.

Lord Wesley's lack of response suggested he'd be here not one moment longer than he needed to be and she was glad that the dinner was to be a formal meal because otherwise she was certain he would have already left. 'Please God, let me be seated next to him,' she whispered beneath her breath, the incantation repeated even as the party were called in to the dining salon, bedecked with candles and small posies of flowers.

Lady Christine Howard took the seat opposite, the smile she offered friendly.

'I am so pleased to be placed near you, Miss Ashfield, as I cannot wait to ask you questions about your prowess in the healing arts. It was always something I was interested in, but have not really had the chance to further.'

'You would be welcome to come to Northbridge and watch me at work...' The words tailed off as Gabriel Hughes came to take the empty seat next to her under the direction of Amethyst Wylde. He looked plainly wary, eyes cold and distant as he pulled out the chair and allowed a great gap of space between them.

'Lady Christine. Miss Ashfield.' The glass he

carried with him was empty and he nodded to the servant behind him to fill it up again.

The skin on his left cheek had been broken by the force of the altercation in the ballroom and Adelaide determined it must hurt a lot for the swelling was still most noticeable.

She glanced away in uncertainty. The earl was plainly not looking for sympathy and neither was he seeking conversation. The silence from him was absolute and solid as he turned to look down the table, three fingers of his left hand beating out a rhythm on the cloth. Marking time. This close she could see that the embossed silver ring he wore was inlaid with a cross of gold. Unusual. Different.

'Do you see many people in your clinic, Miss Ashfield?' Lady Christine leaned forward as she asked the question.

'Many, my lady.'

She knew Gabriel Hughes was listening by the slight tip of his shoulders and the way his hand stilled. 'I have various people from the village who come and buy my potions, though I find just as many want words of reassurance on a particular condition or ailment.'

'Mama is rather depressed with her life at the moment, a result of our failing finances, I think, and Lucien's injuries on the Continent. She now believes we are all fragile and that chaos is crouching around a very close corner. Do you make medicines for those suffering in this way?'

'Indeed I do. My aunt Eloise used to say emotion always has its roots in the unconscious and manifests itself in the body, so I make concoctions to jolt the mind into an alignment with the flesh for those who want to make the change.'

Gabriel Hughes turned at that and addressed her directly, his voice low and a marked crease across his brow. 'Philosophers since Locke have struggled to comprehend the definition and connection of mind and body, Miss Ashfield. Are you implying that you have found the answer?'

A challenge; direct and forceful. Eloise and Jean had been the masters of such discourse and a shiver of anticipation rushed through her. 'I believe every part of our bodies is linked, Lord Wesley, the cerebral and the physical.'

'Is that right? For the life of me and after co-pious reading I simply fail to see how a mental state can causally interact with the physical body.'

'Belief in one's mind is a powerful force for change, my lord.' Adelaide was mindful that conversations all around the table had ceased in order to listen in to this one. 'And while I agree that the conscious experience is on the one hand the most familiar aspect of our lives and on the other the most mysterious, I also sincerely believe that only together can mind and body form a whole to heal.'

'Any living body?' His glance swept the room to stop at the sight of a bumblebee hovering over by the window's glass. 'Does every living thing employ its own consciousness of being?'

'I for one would not discount it.' Clenching her fingers in her lap, she carried on. 'Religion, law and culture have their hands in moulding our thoughts to be…moderated, but I am not so certain that they should be.'

Daniel Wylde at the head of the table laughed and raised his glass. 'I would like to make a toast to the tenets of free discussion and liberal conjecture. Intelligence is a far underrated attribute and it is always welcome here, Miss Ashfield.'

Amethyst Wylde used the following silence to inject her own observation. 'You would like my papa, Miss Ashfield. He is most interested in these sorts of discussions. His heart is his problem, you see, and his mind refuses to accept the poor prognosis of every doctor he visits. With happiness he has far outlived his naysayers and is that not a triumph for mind over matter?'

'I want it to be true and therefore it is?' Gabriel Hughes's words were flat and yet when she looked at him there was a flash of gold in his eyes that surprised her. Hurt and hope had a certain entreaty to them that was easily recognisable for she had seen the same in so very many of her patients.

Was it for himself that he asked these questions? A malady that was non-physical was the only diagnosis that made sense here. Oh, granted, he had cuts all over his face and hands and bruises probably in the small of his back where the bully Murray had lashed out hard, but she knew there was more to it.

The other day in the park when he had placed his hands across her own she had felt his withdrawal.

Panic. Fright. Disbelief.

The Earl of Wesley had bolted for safety and had been running ever since; even tonight placed next to her in close confinement with no chance of an escape he had been wary, the distinctive echo of a personal battle within that was costing him much.

She wished they might talk again quietly and away from the notice of others. She wished he might inadvertently touch her so that the spark of notice she seemed consumed with might again burn and she could relish the mystery of it.

Aunt Eloise and Aunt Jean would not recognise her here, quivering with the want of a man she hardly knew. Lord Wesley was a rake and a womaniser, an earl who wore his clothes in that particular and precise way of a dandy and one who had admitted to having as much of an issue with commitment as she did.

There would be nothing at all to gain by his company and yet here she was in the quiet lull of other conversations turning to him again.

'The philosophy of mesmerism is gaining in traction as a most useful tool in the healing of the mind. I do have some skill in the area, my lord.'

Hell. Was she suggesting that he place his secrets in her trust? Gabriel could not believe it.

'I think I shall pass up such an offer, Miss Ashfield. Even an enlightened healer such as yourself might have some trouble in knowing what is in my mind.'

She nodded. 'Well, if it is any consolation to you it is also my belief that most people can find the solution in themselves if they are honest.'

'Then that is heartening.' He tried to inject as much lightness in the reply as he could manage, but even to his ears the humour sounded cold.

'Reliving a point of memory sometimes helps, Lord Wesley. It opens the mind to further possibility.'

The flash of fire. The slow burn of skin. Henrietta's last quiet words seared into guilt. Her

*hands holding something just out of the reach
of comprehension.*

His stomach turned and he thought for one
wild moment that he would be sick all over the
table, but as Adelaide smiled at him he regained
equilibrium, the warmth of her concern and the
goodness in it bringing back a balance. His heart
might be thundering in his chest, but he remembered again how to breathe. Around them the
chatter of others flowed on unhindered as the
food was delivered to the table in a succession
of dishes.

Chicken, beef and duck trussed in fruit and
heavy sauces and elegantly presented on their
silver platters.

He knew she could see him shaking and knew
also that he should turn away to try at least to
stop her seeing his fear. But he couldn't. Miss
Adelaide Ashfield was his lifeline even in the
cosy private salon of old friends.

'The food is lovely.' Her words and closeness
gave him time to return to the mundane. 'I should
not have imagined putting chicken with flowers
of nasturtium. My uncle employs a French chef

at Sherborne and we are more than used to eating well, but this, well, it is just lovely and I was pleased to get an invitation.'

He made himself smile at her through the haze.

'I am certain you are about as interested in the presentation of food as I am, Miss Ashfield, but I thank you for your effort in distracting me.'

Deep dimples graced both her cheeks and the blue of her eyes was lightened. 'Gratitude suits you, my lord. It makes you look younger.'

At that he laughed and for the first time in a long while felt the tight band of loneliness shift. When the footman came forward with the express purpose of refilling his empty glass he shook him away and took up the jug of lemonade instead.

'I thought Gabriel and Adelaide Ashfield looked good together, Daniel.'

Much later Amethyst Wylde lay curled up against the warmth of her husband and watched the way the moonlight filtered across the strong lines of his shoulders.

'Miss Ashfield was a surprise, I will say that.'

'In what way?' Raising herself on her elbow, Amethyst caught his glance.

'She is clever enough to understand Wesley has secrets and brave enough to try to learn them.'

'She was holding her breath when he looked as though he might very well faint away. I am certain of it.'

Daniel sat up, rearranging the pillows behind him. 'Gabriel thinks the death of Mrs Henrietta Clements was entirely his fault.'

Amethyst heard the worry in his tone. 'He told you this?'

'He has always been complex and I think he has been mixed up somehow in working for the British Service. A few years ago he was easier to read, but now...' His words tailed off.

'Now he hides everything. Like you used to?'

His lips turned upwards.

'He needs a good woman, Daniel, and I think he has just found one. But he does not quite know it yet.'

'Because we men are too...slow to understand exactly what is good for us?' His hand crossed to her cheek and he tipped her head towards him.

'Slow in some ways, but much faster in others.' Amethyst felt his interest quicken as she pressed against him and when he brought her in closer she forgot the conversation completely.

Chapter Nine

Gabriel kept to the shadows as he walked, tucked in against the tall walls of the garden mews. The moon was barely there and for that he was pleased.

A long time ago he had been afraid of the dark, when his father had come home to the family at night screaming and yelling, his fists raised against anyone who might annoy him.

But that was before he had learnt how to use it and make it his own. Now the dark held only freedom and ease. Slipping between the gates, he moved over to one of the downstairs windows.

Friar was inside and talking, for Gabriel could hear the quiet burr of his words. There was a woman present, too, and she did not sound happy.

'No. It cannot be done. He is not a patron of

my establishment any more and I have no way to see to it that he might turn up again.'

'You are a force to be reckoned with, Mrs Bryant. Surely there could be some pleasurable persuasions you could use...'

The sound of notes and coins had its own music. A substantial inducement to comply. Her voice was quieter now, but underlined with the sound of cajoling.

'No.' Friar's shout almost made Gabriel jump and he waited—a single curse and then retreating footsteps. Others had come from further within the house, bringing a light with them, the shadows of movement sweeping across the curtains. Then silence.

Gabriel breathed in deeply and held his body against stone. Immobile. Sensing danger before he saw it as three men with a lantern scoured the yard thirty feet away. The woman had left in the midst of an argument. Mrs Bryant. The voice sounded familiar to him, though he could not immediately have placed the name.

Shuffling along to a small door, he brought out his knife and slid the blade between the fastening and timber. He needed to be out of sight before the men were upon him. When the portal opened he simply slipped inside and sank down beneath the level of the glass at the windows. The flare of light hit an opposite wall and then was gone, returning before fading again into the distance.

Safe for this moment at least. The chamber he sat in was a lobby of sorts, small and rectangular, with a number of doors leading from it. Three pairs of boots sat beside him under a heavy oilskin coat. He wondered whose house this was and why they should be meeting here. Friar's rooms were further west in a far less salubrious area of London.

A long sword in its sheath caught his attention for propped up against the lintel of a door the weapon was patently in the wrong place. He was careful to keep his back against the timber panel as he looked out into the night, glad for black and quiet. He knew he had to get out of here before they came back, but from habit his hands delved into the pockets of the oilskin and came up with a twist of paper. When he heard the returning feet on the wooden floor he left, using the darkness to slip away into shadow and safety.

The note was in French and written on part of a torn map. Alan Wolfe, the head of the British Service, stood beside him as he flattened out the sheet to try to determine exactly what geography it showed.

'Maisy is in the Baie de la Seine. Halfway between Cherbourg and La Havre, the town boasts direct access to the English Channel. We have people in Caen so I will get them up there to look. The writing gives two names: Christian and Le Rougeaud.'

'Napoleon's Marshall, Michel Ney, was named Le Rougeaud for the colour of his hair.' Gabriel frowned. 'Though last I heard he was with Soult in the south of France.'

'Could it be a street, then? Or a description of a place?'

'The name of a boat would make sense, too, bringing things or people to England. Perhaps Christian is the captain?'

And so it went on for an hour or more as they

gathered the possibilities of the intelligence and turned it this way and that.

'No one is there at the address you went to last night. The place is spotless and empty.'

'Then they cleaned up.'

'Which indicates they did not want us to know anything. Did they see you?

'No. But I jimmied the door. Perhaps they found it had been tampered with.'

'You are certain it was George Friar?'

'I am. His accent is hard to miss.'

'And the others?'

'English and French. I would recognise the voices if I heard them again. There was also a Mrs Bryant and hers was a familiar voice.' The Temple of Aphrodite came to mind and he made a mental note to go back and check. Trying to remember the words between them, he tipped his head and then went on. 'A brothel owner, perhaps? She said she had an establishment and Friar said something of pleasurable entertainments.'

'I will get someone to look into that.' Wolfe

took a pen and wrote the names on some paper before laying them on the table.

'Clements has French ancestry and so does Friar by way of marriage. He is also an American and likely to hate the English. Goode is the son of a squire in Leicester, but he is married to a French woman, Lilliana de la Tour. Frank Richardson has written a treatise on the place of free speech and the rights of men.'

'Henrietta Clements swore there were six of them. Clements. Friar. Goode and his wife and Richardson and Mrs Bryant perhaps?'

'Then we need to find proof of what it is this group is trying to accomplish and we need it soon. I will get more men on to the task and hopefully we will be able to round them all up before too long. You look done in, Gabe, perhaps by the numerous social occasions you are at almost every evening. I have heard it said that Mr George Friar is rather enamoured by Miss Ashfield.'

Wolfe looked at him directly as he said it, but Gabriel, with his years of practice, easily hid emotion. He knew the director had heard of his own involvement with the niece of Penbury, for very little of the everyday happenings of London's society seemed to escape him. Wariness made Gabriel swallow. He didn't want Adelaide mixed up in any of this. He needed all the compartments of his life kept separate.

For years he had built up a reputation that was shallow and dissolute. A dandy and a lover was not on anyone's list of needing to be watched and the rumours of a prowess in sexual conquests had kept him apart from those who would discuss politics, government or anarchy.

Hiding in plain sight was rewarding. A certain smile, some well-chosen words, the cut of his cloth and the tie of his cravat. These were his tools now. Innocuous. Harmless. And ready to listen.

The war against France was not always won on the battlefields of valour, glory and blood. It was also fought well in the quiet comfort of bedchambers and in the presence of whispered secrets and willing bodies suspended in the last thrusts of ecstasy when all the walls were let down.

Daniel had called him kind and so had Cressida. But Gabriel knew that he had not been such for a very long time.

He had lived down to his reputation all of his adult life. *Gabriel Hughes, the Prince of Passion.* He'd heard the name in various places, spoken quiet with a hint of disbelief. Such rumour had helped him squeeze between the cracks of the polite and mannered world and on to the warm mattresses of confession.

A gun killed one man at a time, but words smote many. Anarchy and rebellion had shades of truth and honour, too, but as he passed on the names of those whom his paramours had mentioned, Gabriel could not dwell on that.

Sometimes he wondered though. Sometimes he heard the tales of men who were good and true killed by unnamed others, their blood running into the gutters of martyrdom and innocence. The hidden cost of his subterfuge. Yet still he had not wavered.

Until Henrietta Clements. She was just another mark at first, a way to listen in to the nefarious truths of her husband, but she had been lonely and he had been, too, pneumonia laying him low for many months of winter. With his guard down he had let her in, past the point of simply business. They had met on numerous occasions and by then she was dangerous: to the British Service and to him.

At the time of the fire he had even thought Wolfe had had a hand in it, a way of dealing efficiently with every problem, but he had found out later that Randolph Clements had been camped out in the woods near Ravenshill with a group of his men.

Revenge. Retribution.

The strong emotions left little space for caution and Gabriel had been flung from that life into this one.

No one knew the true cost of his injuries. No one. And he damned well meant to keep it that way.

Lucy Carrigan's small afternoon tea party was finally coming to an end and Adelaide was pleased to see her uncle and her chaperon nearby getting ready to take their leave. The débâcle at the Whitely ball seemed now to be a thing of the past, the rumours of Adelaide's personal fortune cancelling out other perceived flaws. Indeed, despite her uncle and Imelda's misgivings, the gossip and disapproval had quickly dissipated.

She had caught sight of Mr Friar earlier in the day and had managed to keep out of his way since then, but suddenly there he was before them as they were making their way to the door.

'Lord Penbury.' He tipped his head and then straightened. 'I did not realise you were here this afternoon, Miss Ashfield, or I should certainly have come over to give you my regards.'

Resisting the urge to answer, Adelaide stayed quiet, hoping that they might leave their meeting at that. But Mr Friar carried on regardless.

'Well, there was also something that I needed to relate to you in particular, Miss Ashfield. A friend of mine, Mr Kenneth Davis, has made it known to me that he was a neighbour of yours in Sherborne many years ago and he wished for me to give you his regards if by chance I did see you in my travels.'

Adelaide's world narrowed and then reformed, the spots of fear in her vision threatening to overcome her completely. Was this a warning? The beginnings of blackmail? She pushed her hair back with a shaking hand and tried to smile even as her uncle spoke.

'The world is a small place, is it not, Adelaide? Kenneth Davis and my niece were once great friends until he hared off to parts unknown in search of a fortune.'

'A fortune?' Friar turned the words on his tongue. 'He lives in Baltimore now, Lord Penbury, and is doing more then well.'

'Such a coincidence, is it not, Adelaide?'

As her uncle offered this opinion George Friar laughed. 'Much of his conversation is about the wonderful time he had as a youth here in England. I think he fancied himself in love with your niece, my lord, and after meeting her I can well see why.'

'He was a wild boy, Mr Friar, and rather wayward. The colonies are probably most suited to men such as him.'

'That they are, my lord, but his stories are most amusing. Perhaps you might allow me your company in order to relate them to you, Miss Ashfield.'

George Friar knew what had happened all those years ago and he knew Adelaide knew that he did. All the horror and fear she felt became entwined in another even more dreadful realisation.

If she refused his suit, for that was obviously what this conversation was about, what might happen next? She could not allow him to see her alone until she could formulate a plan.

The mention of a fortune had caught her uncle's interest, however, and instead of leaving as they were about to he turned with a question in his eyes.

'What is it you do there in Baltimore, Mr Friar?'

'Shipping, my lord. I bring wood from the Americas to England. I also have a large holding on the Jones Falls River in Coles Harbour that I farm, for there are rich pickings to be had if one is willing to work for it and I most certainly am.'

'Indeed. Your family must be proud of your endeavour, then. I always thought my own son should have tried his luck there. Perhaps you might take a turn about the room with Mr Friar, Adelaide. You would probably like to hear about Mr Davis and his new life in the Americas.'

And just like that she was dispatched into the care of Mr George Friar, his hand beneath her arm as he led her around the room.

'I am sorry I did not tell you of my acquaintance with Kenneth Davis at the Harvey ball, Miss Ashfield. I thought it would be nice to get to know you first, to find out for myself if what he said of you could possibly be true. My tripping on that blasted plant put an end to that.'

So he would not mention his own lack of manners? She decided to play along. 'And what was it he has said of me, sir?'

The affable but bumbling tone suddenly changed. 'He said you held one of the richest fortunes in England in your palm, Miss Ashfield, and that if his father had not had him manhandled on to the next boat out of England you would have had to marry him.'

She was pleased that he now showed her his true malice.

'He was wrong in that assumption, Mr Friar.

No woman has to do anything she does not wish to simply because of the poor manners of a suitor.'

Her heart was thumping, but she kept her smile in place and was glad to feel her strength returning. Cover a bluff with a bluff; a cardroom strategy that she'd heard from Bertie.

'Society here needs just to hear a rumour of impropriety to believe it to be true, Miss Ashfield. Especially in a woman.' The cold threat in his voice was evident. 'It is dangerous ground that you are treading.'

'You seem to be ignoring the opposing argument that those who tell tales often come under their own scrutiny, Mr Friar. If it is truly a wealthy wife you want from this visit to England, it would pay you to stay out of such quagmires.'

He took a step back, the smile on his face now overwritten with anger. 'My offer to marry you still stands, Miss Ashfield. I believe we could do well together. The beginnings of a dynasty. And if not...' He left the threat unfinished.'

My God, he believed she would simply surrender to his bullying? Was he mad? 'I will surely think about it, Mr Friar, but for now I need to leave. A headache, you understand.' She brought her hand to her brow and tried to look suitably in pain.

When Friar tipped his head and let her go she knew she had won a short respite at least. Better to let him believe that he was in with a chance than to cut him off completely. Breathing out, she walked towards her uncle, praying all the way that the absolute fury she felt inside would not be showing on her face.

Gabriel fell into a wide leather wingchair at White's and ordered a stiff brandy.

Daniel Wylde sat opposite him, the smoke of a cheroot winding up between them.

'My wife is worried about you, Gabriel. She thinks you are lonely.'

'Lonely for strong wine and shapely women,' he drawled back. The persona he had fostered was so easy to regather in the face of anything personal.

'Lonely in life, were her exact words. She

thinks Miss Adelaide Ashfield would suit you nicely as a bride and has bidden me to raise the subject.'

Speechless for once, Gabriel listened.

'She is wealthy and she is comely. But most of all she is clever and real. A woman like that is rare. Amethyst thinks you are half in love with her already.'

'Love is a strong word, Daniel, and one I have had no practice in at all.'

'Love is the only word that takes away loneliness. Perhaps you should think about that.'

Gabriel laughed, but the sound was mirthless. 'Your matchmaking ability leaves much to be desired. Perhaps if you just stop there we'd both be relieved.'

'It's good to be back in your company, Gabe.'

The quiet honesty of the statement floored Gabriel and he remained silent, fighting back the desire to lay down every one of his problems before the scrutiny of an old friend.

Daniel lowered his voice. 'It is also whispered you work for the Service. Undercover?' He allowed this to settle a moment before continuing.

'Battle was wearying in the Peninsular campaign, but it was usually quickly over. You have the looks of a man who has been under fire for a very long time.'

'God. I do not need this.'

'Don't you? I think you need to hear a new perspective. A perspective that includes a life of your own and a liberty unconstrained by the requirements of a country that will be wanting for ever. The army was like that for me in the end. I came out with a bullet in my leg and nightmares and if I didn't know who I was on decommission, then no one else was ever going to have the chance to, either.'

'A brutal ending?'

'True. But my wife saved me.'

The words dropped across hope, flattening it. No woman would ever be able to save him. He was the most renowned lover in all of London town with a string of conquests to his name and yet he could no longer feel anything.

'You have been dallying with the wrong sorts of women. Cressida Murray was always going to be trouble and so was Henrietta Clements.'

Gesturing to a passing waiter, Gabriel ordered a bottle of fine Scotch.

'Get drunk with me, Daniel, as a friend, and tell me about your horses.'

Chapter Ten

'Are we not besieged by men who are most...
unsuitable, Imelda?' Lord Penbury sighed. 'Run
over by them like a pack of rats on a sinking
ship? Mr George Friar, whom one cannot quite
manage the gist of despite his self-proclaimed
fortune, and the Honourable Richard Williams,
who is afflicted with a dire lack of gumption.
This is not taking into account all of the others
whom my niece dances with once and then never
allows them to enjoy a second turn around the
floor.' He stopped, trying to find the words. 'It is
so much more exhausting than I had ever imagined it to be, I can tell you that. My daughters
were easy to marry off, no fuss, no problems.
They came, they found, they married.'

Imelda joined in the one-sided conversation

now. 'Your niece inspires strong reactions from men and yet she seems to return none.'

'Well, Lord Berrick at least has offered for Adelaide's hand in marriage.'

'When?'

'Yesterday. He came to see me in the afternoon and on speaking with him I can see Adelaide would have much to gain by looking favourably upon his suit.'

'Have you spoken with her about this?'

'No. I do not wish to have another argument and yet…he is a good man and more than wealthy. He loves her and made much of telling me exactly how he does. He is, I admit, very verbose, but he is more than genuine with it and he has promised to allow Adelaide the space and time to pursue the interests that she holds dear. Her clinic. Her tinctures.'

'Then he sounds most reasonable, though your niece might not recognise it as such. The young have no idea of what their future might hold, in my opinion, Penbury, or of how hard the path of life can be. Perhaps we should help her to make the right choice.'

'How?'

'Oh, there are many ways, my dear, ways that have been used for years and years by the wise chaperons of the young and the foolish. A small push here, a larger one there and, *voilà*, the goal is reached easily.'

'You think Lovelace is a fine choice, then?'

'I do. The best Adelaide could hope for at her age and with her attributes. She is outspoken and her independent nature is not one that most men of the *ton* would find appealing. Besides, I knew Frederick Lovelace's grandmother well and she always spoke highly of him.'

Alec breathed out. Subterfuge was a game he shied away from normally, but his niece had brought him to his wits' end. Bertram would return home to Northbridge one of these days with a wife of his own and then children to follow and he worried that Adelaide would feel replaced somehow. Lost in the mêlée of a new generation. No. She needed her own life and house and husband, he was damn certain of it. His brother would have said the same had he still been in the land of the living. John would have encouraged his daughter to spread her wings and find what he had had in his own life, a happy, comfortable marriage. He would be far from pleased to see her grown so alone, and whilst Eloise and Jean had been company for each other in their old age, Adelaide would have no one.

'Do what you need to, Imelda, but do it carefully. I should not want my niece to know that she has in any way been pushed into this.'

Lord Berrick was waiting in the drawing room when Adelaide came down that evening having dressed for the McWilliamses' ball. He looked different tonight, happier, and his clothes were stamped with the impression of much thought and coinage. A good-looking man despite his rather dull character.

'Miss Ashfield.' She looked around for her uncle and for Imelda Harcourt, but they were nowhere at all in sight. She could not believe that this would be considered proper to be left alone together according to the strict tenets of the *ton*. Still, his smile was real and he was so very unthreatening she felt herself relax.

'I am honoured to be asked to escort you to the ball tonight, Miss Ashfield.'

This was the first Adelaide had heard of the arrangement, but she stayed quiet.

'I brought your uncle a book I enjoyed and he has just gone to find one that he recommends for me to take home.'

'You read?'

'Anything and everything. I have no taste, only appetite.'

Despite the situation she laughed. 'My oldest cousin, Cynthia, always called me the family bookworm. When I was younger I used to imagine that literally and worry.'

'Well, my dog almost took a bite out of the First Folio of William Shakespeare the other day and it is worth a small fortune.'

'You have dogs?'

'Three of them. All large and unfortunately rather stupid. But I like them.'

Tonight without the whirl of society trapping them she thought the earl seemed nicer and far easier to speak with.

When her uncle returned with Lady Imelda

a few moments later, she was sitting next to Lovelace on the sofa, talking of the house that he had grown up in. Lady Harcourt quickly fastened on the topic.

'Oh, Thornbury Manor is a very beautiful place. Your grandmother and I used to walk around the lake there and talk and plan all sorts of wonderful gardens that would enhance it.'

'Did they eventuate?' Adelaide was interested.

'Yes, many of them did,' Imelda replied with a smile, 'and I hope you might one day have the opportunity to see them, too, my dear. There is a white garden down by the lake and pinks and reds and yellows at the front of the house. Are they still there, Lord Berrick?'

'Mother did not have quite the green finger that my grandmama did, Lady Harcourt, but if one looks I am certain the ancestors of those plants might still be rearing their heads come the Season.'

'Family,' Imelda purred. 'How important it is and how vital the connections. Do you not think so, Penbury?'

'Indeed, I do. Without the traditions and the

solidarity of kith and kin one would be adrift and alone for ever.'

Adelaide felt the pull of something strange. There were undercurrents she could not understand at play here and she struggled to interpret them.

Berrick smiled wistfully at her, but was all attentiveness. His conversation was not quite as dull as she might have once thought it either, and as the hour wore on she realised she was indeed enjoying herself. Oh, granted, the words were not wit-sharp as they had been at the Wyldes the other evening with Lord Wesley, and when Frederick Lovelace leaned over she was not bothered whether he inadvertently touched her or not. But it was easy and good humoured and for the first time in a while her uncle smiled as though he meant it and looked pleased with her, the genial uncle from Sherborne more apparent.

Family. For all it was and all it wasn't, she enjoyed seeing Uncle Alec happy.

'You have no other siblings, then, Lord Berrick, no cousins?'

He shook his head, the candelabra above catching the gold highlights there. 'None, I am afraid, for my parents were only children in both families. You are lucky, Miss Ashfield, with all your cousins.'

'Well, three of them are a lot older than me and Cynthia and Elizabeth live in the north now. Barbara married a man from Boston and we have not seen her in years. Bertram, at least, resides in London.'

'I should want a large family myself. Sometimes when I was young it was lonely.'

The earl's honesty made her smile. It was rare for a man to admit to such emotion and she lauded him for it, though catching the glance her uncle and chaperon gave each other across the table she stiffened. Knowing. Smug. The horrible thought came that this meeting had more to it than the enjoyment of a simple uncomplicated conversation.

The twelve weeks of the Season that she had promised her uncle were whittling away, yet he had become more and more desperate for her to find a suitor that she held some penchant for. Had he spoken to Lovelace about his hopes? Had he even encouraged the earl?

Berrick himself had no part in it, she was certain. He was a man without the agendas of the more complex males of the *ton*. She almost had to stop herself from leaning over to take his hand and reassure him when her uncle began to question him more blatantly.

'If you were married, would you live in London or at Thornbury?'

'I like the country, sir,' he answered. 'But I think it would depend on what my wife preferred.'

Her uncle's eyes reflected his appreciation.

'And what of travel? Do you have plans to go abroad?'

'No, sir. I have never wanted to leave the fine green fields of England. I have all that I might need here.'

A further benevolent nod from her uncle.

Imelda remained very quiet, but Adelaide felt her chaperon's gaze pinned upon her.

When her uncle suggested they should start for the McWilliamses' ball, she readily assented.

Anything at all to get out of this cosy foursome that was laden with a great dollop of intention and an obvious undercurrent of deceit. She hoped fervently that Mr George Friar would not be attending.

The Earl of Wesley did not ask her to dance, even when Berrick had been called from her side where he had been stuck like glue for most of the night. No, Gabriel Hughes stayed at one end of the salon though sometimes she caught his glance upon her, flat and hard and unreadable. As the music began again Adelaide knew it was a waltz and she looked at Wesley directly.

Come and ask me. Come and hold me close.

The thoughts tumbled forth unbidden and shocking, the force of feeling within surprising even to herself. But Gabriel Hughes simply wandered off towards the top of the room, the tallest man here and the most beautiful, collecting a drink as he did so and never looking back once.

'You look very lovely tonight, my dear.' Imelda's words brought her into the moment. 'I was saying to your uncle how London's society has suited you, made you glow, but never more so than now. Frederick Lovelace looks well tonight, too, do you not think?'

She nodded because her chaperon seemed to expect it.

'He is a man whom many of the other young women here would be pleased to walk out with. Look at Miss Carrigan, for example, she is lit up like a beacon in that waltz with him.'

As she spoke Imelda leaned forward and took her hand. 'The wise choice of a husband is crucial to the certainty of any woman's future happiness, Adelaide. What seems desirable now is often less so when the rosy glow of attraction has lessened.' Her fingers gripped harder. 'And believe me, it will. Pick a man who is rich and biddable would be my advice; one whom you might enjoy the material advantages of, but is happy to allow you to do so. These are two very different things.'

'A man of wealth and weakness, you mean?'

Imelda laughed. 'A woman's strength is all that is needed in a marriage. The position is too crowded should a man expect to have his say, too.'

Adelaide thought her old aunts would have liked Imelda's sentiments, but for her such an argument spoken out loud was jarring. What of equality and the challenge of each other's minds? Where would discussion and debate be consigned to should a union be so very one-sided?

'My Charles and I were wed for thirty years and nary a cross word between us. Lovelace has a resemblance to my dearly departed husband and should I offer you any advice at all it would be to make certain that he understands your more-than-obvious affection for him.'

At that moment the Earl of Berrick caught her glance between the shoulders of others who stood on the dance floor and smiled. A perfectly sweet smile.

'He has offered for your hand in marriage, you know. Your uncle said I was not to say anything, but these things need to be nurtured in exactly the right setting and, if I might presume to say so, I think that this is it.'

Horror coated humour and then anger cloaked

that. This whole evening had been about establishing signposts for the acceptance of a suitable marriage contract. Young women of high-born rank had been tutored extensively in the knowledge of what was owed to the family name and love was not considered an essential element at all. Females here married for security and freedom and wealth and, indeed, who could blame them with the abysmal strictures of manners and formalities attached to innocence.

God, how she suddenly hated the cage she had constructed all of her own making. She should never have agreed to come to London in the first place because the reality of it made her question all she used to believe. Spinsterhood suddenly held as much of a trap as an unhappy union, the length and breadth of aloneness as repulsive as the enforced deceit of an unequal partnership.

Her thoughts fell to Daniel Wylde and his wife, Amethyst. That was what she wanted. The joy of strength in difference and a forged togetherness because of it. Berrick would never give her that.

Her aunt and uncle were plotting a marriage in which she had no say, and Lovelace had already offered his hand. If she did not act now, she might well indeed be married before she knew it and to a most unsuitable groom.

On the pretext of going to speak with Lucy Carrigan, Adelaide left Lady Harcourt and walked further into the room, a vaulted ceiling separating this part of the salon from the next.

She had never thought of herself as particularly brave or desiring of adventure, but tonight everything inside her was different, heightened, alive. Gabriel Hughes stood talking with Lucien Howard, his sister, Christine, next to him, and as Adelaide gave her greeting she was swallowed up into the group with an ease that was both surprising and gratifying.

'I was just saying to my brother how much I enjoyed our evening of discussion the other night, Miss Ashfield, and how we should do it again. Soon.'

'I would like that, Lady Christine.' She did not raise her eyes to Lord Wesley, but felt him there, a solid and startling presence. His shoes were beautifully polished and the cut of his pantaloons a fine one. The damned blush that she seemed cursed with for ever in his presence was beginning to creep into her cheeks.

When Lucien and Christine began to talk to each other of a man they both had just seen, the Earl of Wesley leaned in and spoke quietly.

'Are you well, Miss Ashfield? You seem out of sorts.'

A smile tugged at her lips and she made herself look at him directly, the gold in his gaze questioning. He held the look of a man who did not want to fight any more, wary and drained, but even this did nothing to deter her.

'Would you partner me for the next waltz, my lord?' There it was out, said, blunt and honest.

He was good at hiding things, but still she saw shock on his face and question.

Lost in the consternation of this Adelaide was not cautious with her next words. 'Lord Berrick wants me to marry him.'

It was as if the world around them no longer existed, the people and the noise relegated to a place far away, lost in the ether of what each of them was saying, words under words and the colour of the room stark in only black and white.

Gabriel Hughes stood very still, a grinding muscle in his jaw the only movement visible. 'And what do you want?' he asked finally.

'A home, though it is only recently I have come to realise that a place to be and live is important. My chaperon has been quick to tell me that when Bertie brings a bride to Northbridge I shall be... in the way.'

He turned towards her, using the pillar as a barrier so that they were cut off from the hearing of those around them, but she knew that it would not be many seconds before the world around them impinged again.

'You would be bored to death with Freddy Lovelace in a week.'

'Could we meet privately, then?' She made herself say the words, hating the desperation so obvious within them.

'Pardon?'

'I need to know what it would be like to touch a man who might make my heart beat faster before I settle for one who does not. Your reputation heralds a great proficiency in such matters and I thought perhaps you might...'

'Hell, Adelaide.'

The horror of everything spiralled in her head. She had asked for something so dreadful that even the most dissolute lover in all of London town could not accommodate her.

'I...can't.'

His voice was strangled and rough, the words like darts as she turned on her heels, hoping he did not see the tears that were threatening to fall as she walked briskly from his side.

Gabriel leaned back against the hardness of cold marble and felt pain pierce his chest. The scent of lemon hung as suspended as his disbelief in her words.

I can't.

I can't touch you.

I can't let you know.

She was going to marry Berrick for a place, for a home, for the desperation of not being tossed out of an estate that had always been her sanctuary.

They would never suit. She was far too clever for Berrick and far too...knowing. Adelaide Ashfield would eat a husband like that up in no time flat and be starving for all the rest of her life, doomed to the ordinary.

She deserved rare and remarkable, astonishing and marvellous. The list of adjectives made him smile, but another feeling twisted, too. Sadness and regret. That he had not met her at another time in his life, earlier, when he was still whole, and good and honourable.

'You look pale, Gabe.' Lucien took up the space that Adelaide had just left, his sister, Christine, chatting to a girl he did not know on his other side. 'And Penbury's niece seems upset.'

'I'm tired, that's all.' He tore his eyes away from following Adelaide's form across the room. She was with her chaperon now and her uncle and they looked to be preparing to leave.

He was glad for it.

'For a débutante Miss Ashfield seems to inspire strong feelings in those around her.' A question lingered in Lucien's eyes. 'Selwyn Carrigan was telling me the other day that George Friar was asking after her.'

'The colonial is a charlatan. I hope she stays well away from him.'

'I am inclined to agree with you, for James Stanhope has just returned from Baltimore and he swears he never heard Friar's name or fortune mentioned even once. Strange, one would think, given the importance he accords himself with his land and business dealings there. But perhaps Friar is more than interested in Miss Ashfield's wealth because his own circumstances are not as rosy as he makes them out to be?'

Gabriel frowned. People lied because they wanted things hidden in order to show themselves in a better light and he'd been long enough in the business of secrets to understand the danger in that.

Could the man hurt Adelaide? He had already tried once at the Harveys' ball. Could he do so again? Marriages happened for the flimsiest of reasons and scandal had been the cause for more than a few of the hastily arranged betrothals in the *ton*.

Gabriel did not want Adelaide Ashfield married off to George Friar under a mistake and dragged off into the wilds of the Americas. He wanted her here, to talk with and laugh with, a woman whose conversation he enjoyed and looked forward to with eagerness. Besides that, Frederick Lovelace's proposal was also something to be considered now.

The arrival at his side of Lucien's sister had him turning.

'I have a good friend who would like to meet you, Gabriel. Miss Smithson is new in from the country and she is most adept at riding.'

Smiling, Gabriel straightened the folds of his high cravat and turned to the short blonde-haired woman behind Christine.

The carriage ride home was slow and laborious. Uncle Alec was quiet in his place by the window, but Frederick Lovelace had not stopped chattering. About the weather and the ball. About the moon and his understanding of space. About the scent that she wore and how it evoked for him a time when he had been young.

Adelaide hoped her uncle or Imelda Harcourt might eventually have told him to be quiet or at least to have filled up some of the space with their own opinions, but they did not, and the dreadful monologue droned on and on uninterrupted until they finally reached the town house.

She refused to allow her mind to turn back to the ballroom and to the last look she had of Gabriel Hughes. All she did was smile, inanely, the muscles at the corner of her mouth frozen into the eternally jovial.

'I can't.'

Everything was wrecked and gone. Hope. Joy. Anticipation. When Frederick Lovelace said goodbye she walked quickly up the stairs.

To her room. At last, where she threw herself upon her bed and cried into her pillow, loud noisy sobs stifled by feathers until the slip was damp and cold.

Then she got up and looked at herself in the mirror, the swollen eyes, the broken dreams, the utter sadness of living.

'This is the bottom,' she said to herself in a firm and even voice. 'This is the worst you will ever feel. I promise. It will never again be this bad.'

Gabriel Hughes did not want her. He could not even rouse himself to touch her.

The quiet sound of her heart breaking into a thousand jagged pieces made her close her eyes and simply stand there. Alone.

The next morning her uncle summoned her to his study.

'Frederick Lovelace, the Earl of Berrick, has done you the honour of offering marriage, Adelaide. He came expressly to ask for your hand and I must say that my advice would be to consider his proposal carefully as it is probably the very best you will ever receive.'

Adelaide shook her head and sat down, feeling her legs could not carry her own weight. 'When I came to London, Uncle, I told you that I did not want to be married off to anyone. Those wishes still stand and nothing you say could persuade me otherwise.'

Her uncle was silent for a moment before he crossed to the desk in his library and pulled out an envelope.

'Read this, child.'

Taking the missive from him, Adelaide was startled to see that the writing was in fact that of her late father's.

'John wrote this six months before he died. Our lawyer had insisted we both redo our wills, you see, and so we sat down together and tried to think of all the things we would want to happen should the unthinkable come to pass. Which it did,' he added and laid a hand across her shoulder.

'Your father expected you to marry and have your own family and was adamant that I as your guardian should be the one to help you choose. He was most concerned, you see, for many young women are made unhappy by unsuitable husbands and he did not wish this to happen to you. He wanted a wealthy, sensible, honourable and settled suitor. A man who could keep you in the style you were accustomed. If you look down the page a little further, you will see a list of the families John hoped you to form an alliance with. The Lovelaces are upon it, about the third name down.'

'My answer is still no.' Her words echoed in the silence of the room.

'Are there others there, then, that could take your fancy?'

'There are not.'

'You haven't come across one suitor in all the weeks of the Season with whom you might imagine a future with?'

She stayed silent.

'Then if that is the case, Adelaide, I have failed your father completely. His line shall be pruned into nothingness and lost into the folds of history, for a family tree depends upon regeneration to flourish. If there had been other siblings your choice might have been less important, but there are not. It is only you.' He poured himself a drink and took a hefty swig of it. 'I take this lack as my failure and know that my brother will be looking down upon me and thinking that I could have done more for you, should have done more for you.'

She shook her head. 'You have been a good and loving man, Uncle Alec, and I have felt at home at Northbridge.'

'Well, I thank you for that, my dear, but such sentiments will not solve this tricky situation. Lord Berrick will be arriving back here after luncheon and I had hoped to have been able to give him the Ashfield family blessing, but I cannot force you into sense. Know at least that I tried to deter you from your poor choice of turning away Frederick Lovelace's most kind proposal.'

The words her father had written swam before her eyes. Her parents had loved her and tried to protect her, guiding her from the grave to see her settled in the way they desired. And with George Friar's malevolence simmering unanswered she knew she was walking on dangerous ground.

'I…just…cannot.' Her reply was bare and quiet, and, standing, she placed her father's letter on the table and let herself out of the silent study, hating the deep lines of hurt on her uncle's brow.

Chapter Eleven

Daniel Wylde came again to visit Gabriel in the early hours of the evening.

'I saw Frederick Lovelace this morning. He hopes to have some news of a wonderful new development in his life, I think was how he phrased it. He then asked me if I knew Miss Adelaide Ashfield from Sherborne.'

Hell. Hell. Hell.

The anger in Gabriel twisted into regret and then reformed again into fury. Would she do it? Would she marry him just for a place in the world?

'Lucien said Miss Ashfield looked more than upset after talking with you at the McWilliamses' ball, Gabriel? Is there some problem between you?'

He shook his head. 'The fault was completely my own. She is blameless.'

'Of what?'

I cannot touch a woman without feeling sick.

He actually imagined he might have said the words out loud and his heart began to pound so violently he thought he would fall.

'God, what is wrong with you, Gabriel? Are you ill?'

Everywhere. All over. Sick to my very soul.

'It's the damned Service, isn't it? Is Adelaide Ashfield involved somehow in an investigation?'

You never loved me in this life, Gabriel, not like I loved you...

Henrietta's last words before the fire, plaintive, shaking. He still felt her fingers on the pulse at his neck, nails scraping over the bloodline that flowed there, and the world began to fade somehow into a further-away place. It was coming back, his memory, slowly and by small degrees, little pieces of the past fitting into a whole.

'Sit down before you fall down.' Daniel manhandled him into the chair by the window, the moonlight silver across his lap. 'For the life of me, Gabe, I need to understand what the hell is going on with you.

Sitting, he felt better, more able to breathe and think. Betrayal was all mixed up together suddenly, in Henrietta's neediness and Cressida's revenge at the ball. Even the British Service's insistence on a certain persona to confound those in society held the scourge of it. To him as a person, to his life, to his honesty, to the hope of something better and finer and good.

'After the fire…I lost my way.'

'The fire in the Ravenshill chapel? The one that killed Henrietta Clements?'

'I think she wanted to die.'

'God.'

'I can't remember properly, but…' He could not finish.

'Rumour has it you were burned. Badly.'

Looking up, Gabriel tried to find the energy to hide all he had been so very careful with. 'I was. It isn't pretty.'

'That's why you went to the brothels, then, because of the scarring. You didn't want anyone save the prostitutes to see you like that? Barnsley said you'd been at the Temple of Aphrodite and he wondered if you had said anything of it to me. I told him he must be mistaken because you never used to…' He stopped momentarily before going on, a new comprehension in his glance. 'So the body-and-mind discussion of Miss Ashfield's the other night was more personal than you let on?'

'Leave Adelaide Ashfield out of it, Daniel. I mean it.'

'She talked with Christine Howard of mesmerism…'

'I don't want to hear this.'

'…and self-healing. Of reliving the moment when everything changed and moving on with life. Of coming to terms with what has happened to you?'

The heat crawling across his legs and sending the cloth into flame, skin dissolving as other hands had reached him, pulled him to safety, the last of Henrietta Clements's long hair frizzling into black.

She had smiled at him and then cursed him in

*the last moments before death. 'There won't be
another for you. Only me.'*

The sudden realisation floored him. Gabriel
could barely move with the truth of what he remembered.

'What is it, Gabe? You look like you have seen
a ghost?' Daniel's query came softly.

'I think Henrietta Clements wanted me to die
alongside her. The fire was like a pyre...a sut-
tee. If she could not have me here, then maybe
in the celestial...?' He left the statement hanging
because he no longer had the energy to continue.

'And you didn't remember this until now?
God. Perhaps Miss Ashfield's suppositions about
speaking of a defining moment holds more power
in it than we both gave her credit for. She'll be
wasted on Lovelace if she marries him.'

If...

Swallowing, Gabriel pushed back his fear to
a place where he could manage it. 'Is there any
way, Daniel, that your wife might ask Miss Ashfield to visit your town house again tomorrow
afternoon?'

'Because you want to talk with her?'

'Alone if I can.'

'I think that would be a very good idea.'

Adelaide, accompanied by her maid, Milly, climbed the steps of the Montcliffe town house with a feeling of nervous anticipation. The horror of her dreadful conversation with Gabriel Hughes at the McWilliamses' ball had kept her up for nights and she knew she did not look her best.

The last time she had been here he had been, too, but Lord Wesley was nowhere to be seen as she gave Lady Montcliffe her greeting once inside the front door.

'Perhaps your maid could accompany mine and go and find something to eat and drink in the kitchen, Miss Ashfield. That would give us a small opportunity to talk.'

'Of course.' Milly happily got up, leaving her alone with Amethyst Wylde, who shepherded her into a small salon to one side of an opulent hallway.

'I would like to speak honestly with you if I may, Adelaide…might I call you that?'

'Yes.'

'The Earl of Wesley is a particular friend of ours and he is a good man, a strong man, a man who is misunderstood in society, I think. He admires you. I know that for a fact.'

Adelaide hated the flush of red that had crept up into her cheeks.

'He is here today and he has asked to have a private word with you. Is this something that you might consider?'

Adelaide stood, unable to sit longer. The other day she had asked to meet the earl and he had refused. She could not even begin to imagine what he might want to say now, but it could not get any worse than the last meeting, she was sure of it. And he was here, close. She took in a deep breath. 'I would. My uncle expects me to form a union, but a fortune can be a difficult asset in the marriage stakes, Lady Montcliffe.'

'The rich must marry the rich, you mean?' Amethyst Wylde came to stand beside her.

'Exactly, and Lord Berrick has asked for my hand.'

'I had heard this said, but I do not recall the man himself.'

'My uncle prays for an alliance within the *ton*. My father wanted it, too. There was a letter expressing his hopes for a suitor and his family name was mentioned so...' She stopped, unable to go on.

'Strong persuasions, then. As a way of presenting the other side I might tell you that Daniel was almost penniless when I married him and our union has proved a great success. I think a wise woman can find a way to gain exactly what she wants and make it work, and from what I have seen and heard of you, Miss Ashfield, you are more than up to the task. My advice, for what it is worth, is to follow your heart no matter where it takes you. Now if you will excuse me, I shall find Lord Wesley.'

Adelaide stood in the sunlight by the French doors overlooking the garden, the gentle smell of lemons just discernible in the air. For a moment Gabriel faltered, unsure if what he was about to do was a wrong step or a right one, but then he made himself come forward and the noise had her turning.

She did not wear her spectacles today. That was the very first thing he noticed, and because of it her eyes seemed bigger and much more blue.

Other emotions danced there, too, before she could hide them. Fright. Worry. Joy.

'Miss Ashfield.'

'My lord.'

He did not move closer as he shut the door behind him and when a cloud fell across the sun the room darkened markedly. An omen? He prayed not.

'Thank you for meeting me. I guessed I wouldn't be exactly welcomed at the Penbury town house and so I asked Lord and Lady Montcliffe if they might arrange this. The rumour that you have agreed to marry Lovelace has come to my ears, you see, and—' He stopped, biting down on his babble of words. He was seldom nervous, but here he found he was.

Her smile was sad and it came nowhere near to touching her eyes. 'You of all people should know the danger of listening to gossip.

He was surprised by the ache of relief that went through him at her answer. 'So it is false, this proposed union?'

'Oh, parts of tittle-tattle are always true. Lord Berrick did ask me, but I did refuse him.'

'Because you do not love him?'

'Could not love him. There is a difference. One can marry a man whom one admires in the hope that love might follow, but if there is no feeling whatsoever in the first place, I doubt a satisfactory union would result.' Her voice wavered on the last words, the pulse at her throat rapid.

He covered the distance between them and stood just out of touch, watching the secrets he so often saw dancing in the blue of her eyes.

'You told me once that you never wished to marry at all and that you would like to remain a spinster.'

'And I believed that to be true...then.'

'But now?'

'My place in the world is less certain then it once was and Northbridge is not the home I imagined it to be. I thought to come here for twelve weeks and then return unchanged to get on with my old life, but that will not be so easy now.' She smiled. 'I find myself at a crossroads, Lord Wesley, and it is hard to know in which direction to turn.'

It was her bravery, he was to think later, that made him throw off caution and speak.

'Marry me, then, instead.'

Her mouth fell open and she stared at him, her teeth worrying her bottom lip.

'I am not wealthy and I am not safe in the way your uncle would want a husband to be. There are things about me you do not know and that you may never understand, but I promise to protect you. For ever. My family seat is a pile of burned-out ruins and the town house is heavily mortgaged. But your money should stay in your name, separate to anything I own, because in that way you might understand it is not for riches that I ask this question.'

'Why on earth…would you ask me, then?' Her voice was small, barely there.

'I like the way you reason out things and fight for people and heal them. Besides, Berrick and his stupidity would ruin you and George Friar is not to be trusted.'

The clock ticked in one corner, loud as it measured the passing minute, and outside he heard the rumble of a carriage. Small everyday things counterbalanced against the magnitude of his proposal.

'Yes.'

He could not quite for the life of himself fathom for a second exactly what she meant.

'Yes?'

'I will marry you, my lord.'

'Gabriel. My name is Gabriel.'

'I know.'

Neither of them moved, as though in the action the truth of it all might simply disappear, lost in fantasy.

'Hell.'

She laughed at that, a throaty deep sound that filled the emptiness in him. 'I do not think one is supposed to swear after such a moment, my lord.'

Had she truly just consented to what he thought she had? Could it possibly be this easy?

No.

The answer came quickly. She did not know who he was, what he was, the ache in his thigh only underlining more uncertainty.

He should take the words back and leave her to find her own direction for she had told him of her refusal to marry Lovelace. She was sensible, clever and honest and he was dangerous, unstable and impotent.

Impotent.

The word hung in the air around everything he did and said now and yet he had not been candid with her, with a bride who would know from the first moment he touched her that all was not as it ought to be.

Was this marriage proposal simply selfishness because he thought he might be cured by Adelaide Ashfield's touch? Just another worry that he added to the pile of others.

'I wouldn't stop you doing the things you wanted to. I envisage a marriage of equality and independence.'

He needed to put these things on the table to counter all the other negatives. Perhaps in the balance, then, something could be salvaged, some sense of rightness, and Adelaide had always stressed how important autonomy was to her.

But would it be enough when she came to understand all that he might not be able to give her? He waited for her answer.

'My aunts would have liked you, I think, Lord Wesley, and Lady Montcliffe was just counselling me on the fact that a wise woman finds a union allowing her to gain the things that she needs.'

'And are you wise, Adelaide Ashfield?'

'Wise enough to know that the sort of marriage that you speak of is exactly what I do want.'

She did not mention love or lovemaking.

'I also want a man who I can talk to, a husband who understands the power of conversation and debate.'

Even better. Those things he could manage easily. She neither simpered nor flirted as she stated her requirements, rather he had the notion she had not even thought to. Surprising in a woman. He couldn't help but smile, though a knock at the door brought the others in. His allotted minutes were up and Amethyst Wylde was a woman who was careful with the maintenance of a lady's reputation.

'I hope you have had enough time to settle the affairs between you, Gabriel, but Christine Howard has come to call and I thought we could all have some tea.' Her sharp eyes ran across him as she gestured to her maid to bring in refreshments, a worried look beneath her smile and a hint of curiosity.

'Indeed we have, but perhaps champagne might be more in order, for I have asked Miss Ashfield to become my wife.'

'And she has agreed?' Amethyst asked this question, the timbre of her voice rising.

He turned towards Adelaide, hoping she might say something and was pleased when she did.

'I have.' The soft assent brought Lady Christine to her side, though she, too, was looking at him for more explanation.

Digging into humour, he tried to give it to them. 'The luck of the damned can sometimes take a wondrous turn, though in my defence I have made a concerted effort to explain to my would-be bride all that I am not.' Despite his levity the shock was easily seen on their faces. The anger he felt because of this was palpable. He did not deserve Adelaide Ashfield and they knew it. She was everything good, and honourable and right.

It was Christine Howard who broke the silence. 'Well, I think this is wonderful news. Gabriel has always been interesting and kind. I should imagine he will make a sterling husband and at least with your fortune you will be able to rescue his absolute lack of one. That is two down now. Just my brother and Francis to go and all our problems shall be solved.'

Gabriel had forgotten Lucien's sister's penchant to state the truth in a way no one else would have thought to, though her take on the impending union seemed to have broken through the reserve. As the tasks of finding the necessary things for a toast ensued, Gabriel used the moment to have a quiet word with Adelaide. 'I doubt this news can be contained for very much longer, but if you have any regrets you might be wise to voice them now.'

'Do you?' The query was fired back quickly to him.

He smiled because amazingly he knew that he didn't. 'No.'

'Then why should I?'

'Your uncle won't be pleased.'

'I am no longer a young girl foolish enough to imagine that his opinions should shape my life.'

'But you do understand that others' opinions of me might very well do just the same?'

At that she laughed. 'I hope I am made of stronger stuff, my lord. Allowing others to moderate one's private life is not only absurd, but also very dangerous.'

'And yet the reality of such constant disparagement cannot be overstated.' He smiled. 'Even I find it difficult at times.'

'To live down to your reputation, you mean?' The fire in her eyes was as bright as the small flash of a shared humour. 'Are you trying to dissuade me from your offer, my lord?'

He couldn't lie despite knowing that he should. 'I most certainly am not, Miss Ashfield.'

'Good.' The single word held no hesitation

within it and as Amethyst walked across to join them, a servant behind came with a silver tray full of long-stemmed crystal glasses and a bottle of champagne. Two moments later Daniel was pouring the newly found tipple.

'I'd like to propose a toast,' he said as he finished topping up the last drink. 'To Gabriel and Adelaide. May their union be as happy as ours has been, Amethyst, and as fruitful.'

Gabriel caught the humour on his friend's face as he finished. A quiet ribbing held a certain look and he knew Daniel would want an explanation of events as soon as they got a moment together.

But for now he tipped up his glass and drank, the first hurdle jumped and a row of others in front of him.

The champagne made her feel a little dizzy and Adelaide knew she would have a headache come the morning, but she could also barely believe what had just happened. Gabriel Hughes, the fourth Earl of Wesley, had just asked her to be his bride. The spectres of Lord Berrick, George Friar and Richard Williams faded into the distance as she looked over at the man opposite her.

His hair was queued today, tied back in a severe style, but the cravat he wore was softer. In the light from the window she saw a small scar crossing his left cheek just below the corner of his eye and it seemed to highlight all the danger and risk associated with him.

Yet she could not care. No other man had ever made her feel the way that he did, with his humour and his menace and his manner of speaking that held her in thrall. Even from this distance she could feel the rise of her body towards his, wanting touch and intimacy and closeness. Wanting all the things that a marriage promised, all the things she had for so long been panic-stricken by.

He was beautiful in a way that had her holding her breath and bringing her fists into her sides, the hope of it all overwhelming and irrefutable. Could it possibly be this easy to finally be happy?

In the midst of all the joy Christine Howard a

her side leaned forward to take her hand, squeezing it and smiling.

'I love weddings, Adelaide, and if I say it myself I am very good at knowing what style suits a bride. Amethyst allowed me to help her at her celebration, so if you wish I would be most happy to do the same at yours.'

'I am not…as beautiful as Lady Wylde,' she answered slowly.

'Because you make nothing of yourself. The colours you wear show your skin in a poor light and the style of your hair is old-fashioned and dowdy. But believe me, Adelaide, there is beauty beneath because although you can't see it everyone else who ever speaks about you can.'

'Thank you.'

'You see, there it is, right there. Most women simper at compliments and turn them into something that they are not. Your directness has its own particular allure and Gabriel has been quick to understand this.'

Despite herself Adelaide laughed. 'I would not wish for a big wedding or a very formal one.'

'Amethyst had about four people at hers and

she looked unmatched. Perhaps I could show you her dress and we could begin from there. That sort of style would look very well upon you, too.'

Lady Montcliffe had joined them now and she was smiling as she finished her lemonade.

'I cannot wait until I can have a proper drink again,' she said, her hand crossing the roundness of her stomach. 'From your face, Adelaide, I can guess that Christine is regaling you with her ability to transform one into the most beautiful of brides. From personal experience I should grab her offer with both hands for I don't think I shall ever again look as wonderful as I did on my wedding day.'

'Then I do accept, Lady Christine.'

'Just Christine,' she returned and the three of them set to discussing the colour of gowns and the most flattering ways to fashion hair.

Chapter Twelve

The wedding was small and wondrous.

Her uncle had been furious at first with her choice of groom but had, over the days leading up to the service, made a kind of peace with her that she had found endearing. Imelda Harcourt had simply washed her hands of the situation altogether and left London to stay with her sister in Bath.

'You shall rue this decision for every day of your life, you silly girl, for every single dreadful day. Lord Berrick had a fortune whilst your husband-to-be is rumoured to be a whisker away from bankruptcy. Let us hope he does not fritter your money away as well.'

Those had been the last words between them, though Adelaide had returned to her room to find a book left upon her pillow and inscribed in the front page with Lady Harcourt's name. *Letters on the Improvement of the Mind, Addressed to a Young Lady* was a well-used tome, and Lady Harcourt had marked the section on how to make a good marriage. Each paragraph had stressed the importance of wealth, family name and a spotless reputation.

Lord Wesley had stayed away for the most part. Oh, granted, he had made the obligatory call to her uncle, but the visitation had held only awkwardness, the uncomfortable dislike both men had of the other the resounding tone of the meeting.

Alec Ashfield had made it known from the start that he should have much preferred the suit of Frederick Lovelace for his niece and his questions about the financial soundness of the Wesley estate were both embarrassing and disconcerting.

Gabriel Hughes's estate was in trouble and he made no effort at all to disguise the fact. The family seat had all but burned to the ground and the books of the surrounding farmland accounts were in disarray and confusion.

'You have not been tending to the lands of your ancestors, Lord Wesley, but have instead been cavorting with the womenfolk of London town and gaining a reputation that is hardly salubrious.'

Adelaide thought the earl might argue the fact and was surprised when he remained silent.

'You have the reputation of a flagrant womaniser and a spendthrift and that is discounting your penchant for clothing of a certain style and expense. My niece's money shall not be available to you until you can prove you are a stable and faithful husband.'

Privately Adelaide had wondered if her uncle truly had the power to withhold any of her inheritance, for much of it was already in her own accounts. Still, under the interest of concord, she kept quiet and listened.

'I do not covet Miss Ashfield's fortune, sir, and my finances, whilst nowhere near as healthy as your niece's, still hold a certain robustness. I have not been quite as indolent as you might paint me.'

'My niece is not a woman who would welcome infidelity.'

'I am glad of it.'

'Or intemperate spending.'

Gabriel's smile was quiet, giving Adelaide the impression that he was holding back his fury because this was her uncle and he did not wish for disharmony.

'But as she is twenty-three, soon to be twenty-four, and her choice is obviously made, then I should have to honour that preference.'

'Thank you, Lord Penbury.' This time the Earl of Wesley actually sounded as though he meant it, but he had left straight afterwards, beating a hasty retreat for the front door before she had the chance to converse with him privately.

Christine Howard had also arrived each and every day for the past two weeks. The first visit had consisted mostly of draping various fabrics this way and that, but the second had brought a seamstress who had a quick and deft way with the needle.

'Michelle Le Blanc is Paris trained, Adelaide, and she is one of the best there is. Her husband is a tailor with a firm in Regent Street and as that work is sometimes sporadic she is most appreciative of the extra hours.'

And before long a wedding gown had wound its way out of the light blue fabric, an over-cover of blue-and-green embroidery highlighting the flow of the cloth and a veil in the same thin silk attached to her hair with a band of yellow rosebuds.

Adelaide could barely believe she looked quite so…different. Gone was the girl with a poor taste in colour and design to be replaced by a woman who looked…unfamiliar, her hair flowing down her back and around her shoulders in an artful curl.

'I knew blue would suit you with the colour of your eyes, but I had not quite expected… this.' Christine looked almost tearful. 'If Gabriel Hughes is the most admired male in all of London society, then you shall be his equal in the feminine stakes and none shall question his choice of bride when they see you.'

Crossing the room, Adelaide delved into a drawer of her armoire, bringing out a small box that she had wrapped in a golden ribbon. 'This is for you, Christine. For all your help and generosity.'

When Christine Howard lifted the lid from the box she looked up with a frown. 'Oh, I could not accept such a thing from you. It is far too much.'

The rich red ruby brooch was shaped in the form of a starburst, a number of diamonds alluding to the wake of its movement.

'I saw it in a jeweller on Regent Street and thought of you. It cannot be returned.'

'But it must have cost a small fortune…'

'And since I have a very large one I shall not miss the loss. The man in the shop said it would bring love to the woman who wore it.'

Unexpectedly Christine burst into tears. 'I had love once, but he was killed in Spain. I should not think to ever find the suchlike again.'

Dredging her mind for some words that might help Christine in her loss, Adelaide came up with a line from one of Shakespeare's sonnets,

'"All losses are restored and sorrows end."'

'Do you truly think they can, Adelaide? End, I mean.'

'I do.' Taking the brooch from Christine's shaking fingers, Adelaide pinned it to her bodice. 'And you should, too. There is only so much sadness a person is able to weather in life and you have most certainly had your share. Now it is time for a new direction, a different future. A better one.'

When Adelaide walked up the aisle towards Gabriel Hughes two days later she had no will at all to flee. Lord Wesley was attired in clothes that were almost stark, none of the lace and frills he favoured in society on show, and because of it he looked harder, more distant and larger.

He tipped his head as she joined him, though he did not offer his hand for comfort. The lace and silk of her dress glowed in the light, the full skirt falling in swathes to the floor, the silk almost alive in its movement.

An organ played somewhere close by, the music lilting and sombre. Two large vases of white roses stood to each side of the font. When she breathed in Adelaide could smell the scent of them and it calmed her.

This was the place her parents had been married in and her grandparents before that, the small chapel a reminder of history and permanence.

Her uncle held her elbow firmly and waited until the minister spoke, releasing her into the company of her husband-to-be only after she looked at him and nodded.

'Who gives this woman to be wedded to this man?'

'I do.' Not said in quite the way she might have wished, a flat anger running under the sentiment. For a moment she thought that her uncle would not step away, but then he nodded his head and retreated.

The guests were not numerous, she had seen that as she came in. Her cousin Bertie sat on her side of the chapel with her uncle's older sister. On Gabriel Hughes's side Lucien, Christine, Francis, Amethyst and Daniel Wylde filled the front two rows. Gabriel's mother was there, too, the grey of her hair matching the steely fabric in her gown.

His immediate family was as decimated as hers, Adelaide thought and stood straighter. She usually towered over other men, but with her husband-to-be she almost felt small. Through the gauze of her veil the room was muted, the others further away somehow, just her and Lord Wesley and the quiet voice of the minister as he took them through the vows.

'Do you, Gabriel Stephen Lytton Hughes, take this woman, Adelaide Elizabeth Ashfield, as your lawfully wedded wife…?'

She had seen his names on the marriage contract, but to hear them said here was different. She knew so little about him: his family, his hopes, his truths, his past.

'I do.'

There was no hesitation in his words, no underlying uncertainty. He gave his reply quickly as if he wanted the minister to get on with the vows and have them over.

It was some consolation.

The ring he placed on her finger was also a surprise. Of a Renaissance design and fashioned in gold, enamel and diamonds, the fragile band fitted perfectly. She wondered whom it had belonged to, but he did not linger in his touch or meet her gaze as the circle slid into place. His own hands were bare today, save for the ring she had placed there, no sign of the ornate silver-and-gold band he often wore. It was if she were marrying a stranger dressed in dark and sombre clothes, just a touch of fine linen at his sleeves and neck. None of the man in society on show with the frilly embroidered sleeves and the ornately creased cravats. Even his cufflinks were of plain dark onyx, the stone reflecting none of the light that seeped in through stained-glass windows.

His long hair had been fastened at his nape with a leather tie, the deep red and lighter browns dulled under a lotion that held it in place.

'You may now kiss your bride.'

The minister's direction cut through all her thoughts and brought Adelaide back into the moment. But Gabriel Hughes merely shook away the offer and turned. Catching the worried glance of Amethyst Wylde, Adelaide followed him out.

Could this union be a farce, a travesty, a reminder of all she had promised herself never to feel? It was as if at that moment Eloise and Jean stood just behind her and shook their heads in sorrow.

We told you so, but you would not listen.

Even the spectre of Kenneth Davis could be brought forth and imagined, crouched in the corner shadows with his innuendos and evil. She also wondered wildly what George Friar might make of her sudden betrothal when he knew of it and if that would create a further problem. Had she not promised to give him a reply to his proposal, after all?

'Are you well?' Her husband's voice cut across dizziness.

'I am fine, thank you.' The formality of it all was disturbing. They were married, but they barely knew each other. *Marry in haste and repent in leisure*; the words of the ditty turned in her head again and again and again.

Gabriel Hughes's voice cut through her lethargy. 'My mother would like to meet you. She has just returned from staying with her sister in Bath. But be warned she can be...rather distracted, I am afraid.'

The dowager was a small lady, the corners of her lips turned down into deep creases.

'Mama, may I present Lady Wesley. Adelaide, this is my mother, the Dowager Countess Wesley.'

The older lady's hands were cold and she shook slightly, as though a draught cut through the warm room to land only on her, but the squeeze of ancient fingers was unmistakable as the dowager leaned forward.

'I was more than surprised by this marriage, but Gabriel needs a friend and I hope it will be you. If it was, I could die happily as my daughter has been difficult and I never know quite what will happen with her—'

The earl cut his mother off. 'Perhaps we might all go home to the town house now, Mama. I know Mrs Peacock has done herself proud with the wedding breakfast.'

The wedding meal was a large one, six courses and all served on generous trenchers themed with objects pertaining to a wedding, and when

Gabriel stood to talk he kept things impersonal as he addressed the small gathering.

'Thank you for coming and enjoying this day along with us and a special thanks to Lord Penbury for allowing me his niece's hand in marriage.'

He turned then, his pale gaze running across her. 'Thank you, too, Lady Wesley, for agreeing to marry me and I hope our union shall be a long and happy one.'

Raising his glass to her, he proposed a toast. 'To Lady Adelaide Wesley.'

At least in strong drink some of the reasons for this marriage might be made less obvious, she thought, as she finished her glass, watching as a servant stepped forward to fill it up again. Her agreement to marry Gabriel Hughes was not quite running away from the worse alternatives presented, but at that moment it felt awfully akin to it.

Lord Wesley had not truly looked at her during the whole ceremony save when he had placed the ring on her finger and even that he managed to execute with only the briefest of contact.

He regretted this marriage, she was sure that he did. Oh, granted, her gown was wonderful, the blue bodice clinging about her waist and hips before flaring out on to a full skirt of colour.

Beneath the silk was a satin petticoat, sleek against the wisp of stockings. Christine Howard had dressed her hair in a style reminiscent of the old Grecian gods, fastening at the back of her head in ringlets and ribbons, a half veil attached on rose buds.

She felt beautiful. She did. But Gabriel Hughes had made no effort at all to touch her, even inadvertently.

No, rather he had spent the whole of the day moving away, creating distance, allowing others to stand between them and barely talking.

Even his mother had observed her in pity as the older woman had retired upstairs earlier and Amethyst Wylde had looked at Adelaide sternly as she had taken her hand on their leaving.

'I hope that your union will be every bit as fulfilling as my own, but if you should ever need an ear to listen or a quiet place to talk you only need to send word.'

But.

The word qualified everything and the deep frown between Lady Montcliffe's eyes saw to the rest.

And then everybody was gone, the busy work of servants the only noise left as her new husband drew her into a small salon to one side of his town house and closed the door.

'I need to talk to you Adelaide. In private.'

Chapter Thirteen

He didn't speak as he stood there, running one hand across the back of his neck as though easing an ache. When the silence lengthened she sought for words herself.

'The flowers in your house are all beautiful.'

Another bunch of white hothouse roses stood on the table to one side of the room.

He glanced across at them and then back at her, clearly having other more important things on his mind. His eyes were so unusual, Adelaide thought, the gold of them traced in darker green around the edges. He had broken his nose at some point in his life, for the bridge of the bone was closer to the skin there, giving his beauty a more menacing air.

'Thank you for marrying me.' His words were quietly said.

'You thought that I wouldn't?'

'I know you have heard many rumours about my past, so…' He didn't finish.

'The ones that elevate you to a lover of some note?'

He laughed unexpectedly and the sound made things easier, less formal. 'Well, perhaps not that one, but there are others.'

'Mr George Friar made certain that I knew of a law case in which a woman of your acquaintance had been killed.'

'I see. And he told you it was my fault?'

'I do not think he likes you so…yes, he did. I have heard other things about you, too. It seems you are a man who inspires gossip.'

'Yet still you married me, knowing this and despite all those who were lining up to court you?'

'Well, that queue had shortened somewhat after the Whitely ball when you were hurt.'

Again he laughed, but she was tired of skirting around their situation.

'My wedding ring fits perfectly.' Looking

down at her left hand, she straightened her fingers to where the Renaissance gold glinted in the light. Could this marriage ever be the same?

'It was a family heirloom of my grandmother's. She gave it to me a long time ago and said I was to keep it safe for the wife I would choose. At the time I wasn't sure I wanted a reminder of such permanence, for at seventeen you have such a notion of yourself that everyone else is excluded.'

Adelaide smiled. 'The first time I ever saw you Lucy Carrigan told me that you were the most handsome man in all of society and that the place in which you lived had mirrors on all the walls. To look at yourself from every possible angle, she said, because you were so beautiful.'

'I doubt you would have wanted anything else to do with me if that was the case.'

'Yet there is some truth in what she was saying. Your clothes. Your manners. In society you are a man I barely recognise, but here…?'

The gold of his glance slid away and he turned towards the window.

'I have lived in the shadows for a long time,

Adelaide. Now I find myself wishing for something else entirely.'

'The shadows?' She wanted to know what he meant by that word. Brothels? Gambling halls? Drinking parlours?

His eyes lowered and met hers directly. 'I work for the British Service as an Intelligence Officer and have done so since I was eighteen. My life has not all been indolence.'

Adelaide's mouth dropped open. This was the very last thing she thought he might tell her and yet it all made perfect sense: a camouflage to disguise the truth.

'You are allowed to confess to the doing of such a job?'

'I couldn't before, but as you are my wife now...'

'So that was how you were hurt?'

'Pardon?'

'Your left hand is scarred on the top. It has the look of a bullet wound?'

He raised the appendage to survey the damage before frowning and looking away. 'My mission for the British Service was to ferret out information that could be important. Great things that might change the course of history are hard to come by, but tiny clues and small pieces of information glued together can be as valuable.'

His injured hand lay against the window now, fingers splayed out against the glass, parts of his skin almost transparent in the light, though the scars were darker.

'You were on the Continent with Daniel Wylde? In the war on the Peninsula against Napoleon?'

He shook his head. 'There were secrets in London that were far simpler to shake out than those on a battlefield or with force. A woman unhappy in her marriage, a letter that was left unfinished, a drawer that could be unlocked to find the telling remnants of anarchy. With my reputation access was always easy...'

'The persuasive gentle arts?' she returned. 'And you are good at them?'

'Too good,' he whispered back and in those small words she understood with clarity what the subterfuge had cost him. Living in lies, secrets and deceit had had its own price and Gabriel

Hughes had paid heavily for it. The darkness beneath his eyes alluded to such a penalty.

'I shouldn't wish for a husband who was…unfaithful even for the cause of King and Country.' She hated the way her voice shook, but she was shocked by his candour and the way he could confess to these sins with barely a backward glance.

'Good, for I do not work for the Service in that capacity any more. After the fire…' He stopped.

'You were too visible? Less able to hide?'

Another truth flickered in the gold and this time it was one she could not quite fathom.

'I have not been a saint, Adelaide, or a man who has made all the right choices. But sometimes the information that I uncovered saved innocent men and women and I am at least glad for that.'

He had not told her the whole story, but for now it was enough.

Mirrors and shadows. Lucy Carrigan's ruminations had had a deal of truth within them, figuratively at least. He lived through each day seeing a version of himself reflected in the eyes of others that was as unreal as it was precarious. His life. For years.

No one had had the chance to know him before he was gone again, lost in the translation of services to the King and spiralling into a desolation that was all encompassing.

He had thought he would never get back again, never sleep again, never smile or marvel at the world or a woman whose mind he could see working even as she stood across from him.

'I married you for salvation, Adelaide.' The words dried in his mouth even as he whispered them.

But she had heard for her eyes widened, bluer than the sea and as clear.

'So in essence you are telling me that your reputation with women stems from business rather than from pleasure?'

'Much of it was a smokescreen. A simple kiss, a few well-chosen words and they were happy.'

'A far more tepid version of the exploits whispered about you in society, my lord?'

Gentle humour crossed into her face as his

laughter filled the room, rusty from a lack of use, but there nonetheless. He felt the tension of the last hours begin to unloosen and reform into something else entirely.

He was not the man he had once been, not the man all of London town spoke about as he passed. But the lack of feeling in one part of his body did not exclude his finesse in others and his wife was the most beautiful woman he had ever had the pleasure of knowing.

God, he was stuck in a limbo between want and ability. But he had his hands and head and body still and if he went slowly, following more than just the questionable tenets of lust, who was to know what might happen.

Without his senses trained on jeopardy and deception he could hear the birds singing in the line of trees across the road in the park. He could smell the lemon on Adelaide's skin as well, a soft and lovely scent that came to him as she moved, small wafts of promise.

Life flowed on, after disaster and deceit, after loneliness and dysfunction, after sorrow and guilt.

Tomorrow they would leave for Ravenshill and for the chance at something more, though the shattered remains of the Manor felt synonymous with his own destruction.

He could rebuild. All of it. A better life. A more honest one with a wife whom he admired. But it was up to him to find the way of doing so.

'I hope I will be enough for you.'

God, now why the hell had he said that? It was the lack of being able to touch her, he supposed, and the desperate want that accompanied such a prohibition. If he had been braver he might have simply strode forward and taken her in any way that he could. With his hands and his mouth and teeth if his body would not rise, just to assuage the fury that held him bound and trussed like a slave.

He wanted to see her. He wanted to hold her gently on the generous sofa behind them, late-afternoon sunlight on the velvet, warmth in the room. But already the sweat was building on his brow and the blood pumping in his throat, and if he could not clamp down on the fear then she would know. All of it. His lack. His sins. His guilt. His penance.

'I tried to warn you before of some of the things that I wasn't.' Breathing in hard, he brought his body into check. 'But honesty has its shades, Adelaide. The honesty of a saint? The honesty of a sinner? One person's truth is another's lies, and who has the wit to tell where the lines get crossed or blurred?'

He could see her mind turning as she reached for an answer.

'My old aunt Eloise used to say there are three things that cannot be hidden: the sun, the moon and the truth.'

'Buddha.'

'Pardon?'

'It is a teaching from the time of the Magadha Empire. Buddha penned it.'

'I did not know that.'

He smiled. 'Perhaps truth is only simple. In the end, there it is. Us. Here. Married.'

Adelaide breathed out, his stillness confusing, but beneath the mask of indifference she could see vulnerability there, too, crossed with an ever-present danger that was so much a part of him.

His hand came forward and he took hers, the fingers warm and strong. She felt him take in a breath, too, as he waited, the frown above his brow deep. The pulse in his throat was fast and his fingers trembled.

Not quite as indifferent as he might make out, then, as the same shock of knowledge she felt each time they touched shimmered between them.

'You are warm.' His words were soft, barely there as his forefinger began to trace a pattern down the side of her right thumb, the circles leading to her palm and then into the hollows at the base of each finger; a slow and calculated message of intent. *This is me. This man. Take me if you dare. I am not perfect and I do not pretend to be.*

Challenge, too, surfaced beneath the deliberate. Did she feel what he did? This violent jolt of connection?

She felt her own breath catch and then hold with a rush of blood and flesh. Each time he stroked the feeling went deeper, linking with other echoes, as her body answered with a will all of its own.

Meeting his eyes, she understood, too, that he knew exactly what it was he was doing, a lesson in loving from the master of the trade; both eloquent and disturbing.

When his head dipped his grip tightened, the arch of his neck exposed as his teeth and tongue joined his fingers. The wetness was hot and then cold, smooth and then rough, the sharp pain of his teeth against utter gentleness. Playing her.

Adelaide shut her eyes and just felt. Him. There. Against her. Close. He took her thumb into his mouth and sucked, lathing hard against the tug of want and need, the heady clench of surprise rushing through her as his arms brought her in.

And then quiet. Peace. The true relief of her body.

She could not move, but stood, curled into his embrace, spent and formless. Her tears were unexpected, falling against the snowy whiteness of his shirt, darkening the linen.

Unbelieving and astonished. Why had she not heard of this before, this perfect splendid gift? Why had not other wives told her of it, time and time again? They should be shouting it from the rooftops and from the bedrooms all over London town. Another darker thought surfaced.

'This is what you spoke of. Before? Your job at the British Service?'

Her words were out, said. She could not take them back or rephrase them even as his reply came quick and flat.

'A woman's body is a temple, Adelaide. Every worshipper should give his thanks in the very best way he can.'

The very best...

He was known everywhere for his prowess and for his mastery. So many people had told her of it. His flair in the bedroom, his talent with the feminine sex.

Yet he stood there as if what had just happened was a mundane, ordinary, everyday occurrence for him. He was not even breathing fast now and his withdrawal was obvious.

'Thank you.' She couldn't dredge any other thing from the shocking truth of it.

And then he was gone. A quick goodnight and gone, a servant dispatched to show her the way up to her room.

She thought it a game, then, a pretence. His insides ached from the intimacy. As he reached the gardens to the back of the town house, he sat abruptly on a stone seat so that he did not fall.

He had managed it, just, managed to keep himself safe in the illusion of distance. His hands went to his pocket and he found a cheroot. It took him three times to flint the match and hold it to the end, so badly did his fingers shake.

God. Breathing deeply, he held the smoke inside, the tobacco giving an edge to fear and dulling it into something that was bearable.

He had touched her, with an attempt at the sensual and the promise of what had been in him once. A start.

But the truth had a way of striking back no matter how honestly you phrased it and now Adelaide thought him false, a lover that all of

London had some knowledge about and one who used his art like a weapon.

When he felt a little steadier he stood and walked out into the oncoming darkness through the gates to lose himself in the dusk, as he always did when he was lonely or worried or the world had turned on its tail once again and left him reeling for the sense of it.

He had felt the spark as he had touched her, as staggering as the last time even though it was hoped for...expected. Closing his eyes, he tried to drag the feeling back, the smell of her, the satin of her skin and honesty.

Adelaide.

His wife.

Oh, the demons circled still and close, bound by regret and guilt and wrongdoing, but for the first time in years he felt himself being pulled back in the right direction, back into life.

He had been so out of step with it for so very long, the nights of sleeplessness leading into long days of haze. But here at this moment, he thought, he could have laid his head down and slept. Before the dawn. At a proper time. Creeping back into normality.

'Please,' he whispered, 'let that be.' He did not know if it was to God himself or to Adelaide that he addressed his entreaty and as a growing wind caught him up into its coldness he struggled for all that had been lost inside him and all that he hoped to find again.

She had slept badly, though the room she had been allotted was beautiful. Shelves of books graced one whole end of the chamber and the titles had amazed her.

Eclectic was the word that came to mind. The playwrights Félix Lope de Vega and Miguel de Cervantes sat beside lesser-known poets from the same land. Did Gabriel Hughes speak Spanish, Adelaide wondered, given he had the ownership of a great number of books in that language? Looking down to the next shelf, she lifted up a weighty tome containing many maps of France. His initials were penned inside. Under the writing a date was scrawled: 1794.

Sixteen years ago. Her husband had said he

was thirty-four years old on one of the first occasions she had met him and this evening he had confessed to being eighteen when he joined the British Service.

Was this book from that time, the dog-eared pages attesting to a good use? Had he travelled there to get to know the lay of the land, the contours of an enemy?

Other books about distant wars lined a further shelf. Below that *The Canterbury Tales* and old medieval stories were stacked and in the next shelf down every book was in French.

His initials were inside these ones, too, and passages were underlined neatly as though a ruler had been used to hold them there. Thin tomes of poetry sat beside more ornate manuscripts depicting the flora and fauna of both France and England. Two or three grimoires of witchcraft and sorcery stood next to them.

Gabriel Hughes was a man of wide tastes, then, and an eclectic general knowledge. No wonder his conversation was as interesting and broad.

His honesty tonight had shocked her, but it was

her reaction to his mouth across her fingers that had unsettled her more.

She had wanted him to find other places on her body to caress, too, her mind knowing one thing and her body another. She imagined all the women who had spilled their secrets in the ecstasy of his ministrations, betraying family and spouses for the simple need of touch. My God, she would have done so herself. She would have told him everything had he asked. Her past. Her hopes. Her opinion of their marriage. She had no defence against such expertise and he had not even kissed her or taken her to bed. A blush of desire filled her cheeks and she walked to the mirror to see a woman there she did not recognise, eyes wide with the promise, cheeks flushed in hope.

Honesty.

What had he said of it?

'I think the truth is only simple. Us. Here. Married.'

So simple she could let go of every single truth she believed? Gabriel Hughes had played women false for years now and if the question was whether he'd done so for a greater good or for a lesser one she had no way of knowing.

From the very first second of seeing him she had felt a connection, solid, hard and surprising. It had shocked her with its intensity then and it had grown ever since. Unable to be fought. Absolutely undeniable.

It was why nothing else had felt right ever since: her suitors, her home at Northbridge, her vocation of healing and her acceptance of spinsterhood. She had been thrown into a reality unlike anything she had ever expected, bright against dull, heat against cold, and the truth of it all had led her here. Gasping for breath.

She wiped away the tears that fell across her cheeks in an angry motion. Crying was not a part of it. She needed to understand Gabriel Hughes and allow him to understand her. He had tried to be truthful and she had thrown it back in his face. A lover of repute who could bring any woman he chose to climax, the deceit of it all excused by the intelligence he gathered. Understandable. Even lauded. She knew wars were not always fought on a level playing field and that the compilation of secrets was never going to be tidy, the currency of duplicity having its own payments.

He had not come to her door last night after they had spoken. Neither had he sent word this morning to ask if she would join him for breakfast. Perhaps he, too, was licking his wounds and trying to find a pathway, back to togetherness.

When she finally got down to the dining room he had eaten and gone. To make the arrangements for the trip up to Ravenshill Manor, his butler had assured her and turned away. She had seen the look of consternation that had crossed his brow, though, and wondered at it.

Servants knew everything. She had discovered that fact years ago when her aunt Josephine had lost yet another baby and the silence of grief filled Northbridge. A stillbirth this one and a boy. With hair the colour of moonbeams and perfectly formed despite his early coming and his lordship sobbing inconsolably, behind his desk in the library. Adelaide had overheard her maid talking to another of the upstairs girls and was surprised by the extent and breadth of their knowledge of events. Like a grapevine entwined on to itself as its runners lengthened and thickened.

The Wesley staff would know that Gabriel and she had slept separately and that they had not sat together for a first breakfast, either. Even Milly, who had come with her from Northbridge, had looked tense as she pulled Adelaide's hair into a chignon with draping curls around her face.

'His lordship went out early, mistress, before the sun even rose and I have heard it said he was not in bed either till late. The maid who does the fire grates said he often did not even come home.'

'Perhaps he has commitments, Milly?'

'Commitments, my lady?' Her eyebrows had shot up into her hairline. 'I would have hoped you were the commitment he honoured.' Laying down the brush, her maid caught her glance in the mirror. 'I am sorry, ma'am. I should ha' held my tongue. He is good to his horses if that is any consolation. Tom, the stable boy, told that to me yesterday.'

Adelaide smiled. In Milly's world a man who

was kind to animals could do no wrong at all. She was glad for the information though, for already she had started to worry. If he did not come home night after night, what could she do about it? This was not a love match. Gabriel Hughes had married her out of pity, she thought, or even expedience, her fortune a way to rebuild Ravenshill Manor. She was a salvation, too, a beacon in the darkness he had fallen into.

The problem was that as much as she tried to convince herself her marriage was one of convenience for both of them, other things surfaced to make nonsense of the notion.

The way he had kissed her hand for a start last night, all her senses rising to the surface like water boiling in a pot, the heat and want unstoppable.

The way she saw the sadness in him, too, when he could not quite hide it, his pale gaze lost in other harsher times. Or his ruined right hand when he rested it on his thigh in a way he often did, rubbing it up and down across the fabric of his trousers as though the skin underneath troubled him.

Nay, if she were honest she had wedded Gabriel Hughes because she wanted more. More conversations, more of his smiles, more of the laughter that came quick when she spoke to him of ideas and books and dreams. She had never felt this before with anyone, a sense of kinship and knowledge, the mystery of him wrapped in hope. And need, too. Her aunts had always dismissed that part of a woman, the place that found magic in intimacy. Granted she had, too, for a very long while after Kenneth Davis's attack, but lately some other understanding had budded and blossomed. She wanted to feel his warmth upon her, the urgency, the thrill of blood coursing across reason when he touched her.

The new morning lit the patina of the walls in the breakfast room, the old paint chalked into lighter squares where paintings had been removed. The gentle stroke of penury, hidden under excess. In society it was not what you were but what others perceived you were that was tantamount.

And Lord Gabriel Wesley was the most perfect example of all. Lost in shadow, but bathed in light.

He needed rescuing. He needed trust. He needed honesty. And as his wife she was damn well going to give it to him.

Chapter Fourteen

She had finished her breakfast already. Gabriel saw that as he walked into the dining room and sat to one end of the table, waiting until the servant had brought him his usual plate of eggs and bacon before he spoke.

'I hope you slept well, Adelaide.'

She looked around to check the positioning of his staff before she answered him.

'I have heard that you did not, my lord.'

His fork stopped as he lifted it. 'I seldom sleep for long.' He wondered which servant had leaked out that information. All the stakes heightened again, a wife who might wish to know all the things he'd told no one.

'Do you walk, my lord? Walking helps, I find.

In the country I take a long walk every morning and it allows me the time to think.'

'You are full of excellent advice, Lady Wesley. Perhaps I should indeed start.' He wished he could have made that sound a little kinder, but the few hours of slumber he had finally managed were not enough to foster good humour. He needed to arrange the journey up to Ravenshill and his mother had been ill again in the night. Her health was failing, he had known that for a long while, but today of all the days he just did not have the temperament for her constant melancholy and complaints.

He needed to get to Essex with his new wife. He needed space and time to adjust to being married. He could not leave Adelaide floundering in the no-man's land of celibacy for ever without allowing her some honesty at least as to his reasons.

She was looking down now at her empty plate, her hands in her lap and a frown across her brow. Irritation, he thought. Or uncertainty. The bright and quick mind that he admired lost under the weight of their awkward union and he felt guilty and wary over it.

With a considered motion he lay down his eating utensils and stood, swigging down a mouthful of freshly poured tea as he did so.

'Could you come with me to the library, Adelaide? I have things I need to say to you.'

Another flash of concern in blue, though she nodded and did what he asked, following him down the short corridor. He shut the door the instant she was inside and gestured to a seat over by the window.

'I would rather stand, I think, my lord.'

'Very well. Will you have a drink?'

'This early in the morning? No. Thank you.'

'Would you mind if I did?'

She didn't answer that, but her frown told him she very much would mind. Still with the promise of shoring up his own courage he made certain to pour himself a generous brandy and downed much of it in one swallow. The liquor burnt a fiery path back to valour and he was glad for it. He had to stop drinking so much, he knew he did, and at Ravenshill he would make a start.

'I have not slept well since the fire.'

That was honest enough. He had not done any-thing with any true skill since, but this wasn't the time for that particular confession.

'Have you tried massage?'

The sort of massage the Temple of Aphrodite was famous for? he thought wildly. The type that led to more than just a gentle touch of skin?

'No.'

'My aunt Eloise was an expert. She had a tutor from the East on the subject and people came for miles to have their aches and pains eased.'

Pushing back her sleeve, she laid a finger over a point a little way up from the wrist on her right arm. 'This is *Nei Guan*, a place known to calm the heart and the spirit. With stimulation it can lead to better sleep and is well known, too, for its quelling of anxious thoughts.'

He began to laugh despite trying not to, the guarded tension in his shoulders relaxing with the humour.

'Your aunt taught you this?'

'Indeed, sir, she did.' The words were given back to him without arrogance or pride and the floor beneath him seemed to tilt slowly to one side as he understood what that meant. She was not like any woman he had ever met before, neither boasting nor subservient. She just was. Herself. Different. Unusual. If Adelaide insisted she knew a method of Chinese massage that could put a grown man into the way of sleep, then she probably did.

Finishing his brandy, he placed the glass down on a table beside him.

'I have not the time to try it now, but perhaps at Ravenshill Manor...'

The smile she gave him back made him want to tip caution to the wind and simply tell her everything. But if he did that here in London she might not be willing to journey with him up to Essex and he wanted her to himself and alone with more of a desperation than he could believe.

'We will be departing for the Wesley family seat in a little over two hours as there is word of a storm coming and I don't wish to be caught in it. The house itself has been badly damaged, you see, but has a wing that was left untouched and I sent instructions to the servants yesterday to have it readied.'

'It will just be us…?'

'Yes.'

He saw her take a deep breath before she nodded and, not wanting to have any further argument, Gabriel bowed formally and left the room.

Her husband did not share the carriage, but rode on his large horse beside the conveyance, one of his servants alongside him. Outlined against a leaden-grey sky and with his heavy cloak whipping in the wind, he looked like a figure out of a book: dark, brooding and beautiful.

She'd known he was a good rider back in London, but here on the rough pathways and the undulating hills she saw the true expertise. Horse and man seemed as one flying across the grassy countryside, the sleek pull of muscle and the easy motion of speed.

'I have never seen a gentleman ride like that in me life, ma'am.' Milly beside her leaned forward, watching the earl and smiling. 'If he was unseated…' She left the rest unsaid as Adelaide looked away. She had been enjoying the spectacle until then and wished her maid had not reminded her of the danger.

'It cannot be far to Ravenshill Manor. Lord Wesley said it was only a few hours and we have been travelling all of that, I think.'

'Tom said the drive into the property was lined in oaks. He said in spring the green reminded him of Ireland and of the little folk and that there is not a sight more beautiful in all of the land.'

'The boy in the London stables, you mean? That Tom?'

Milly blushed and made much of finding something in a large reticule she had brought along with her.

Adelaide was astonished. Her maid had been with her for a good number of years and she had seldom seen her embarrassed. But before she could form a question the shout of the driver alerted them to a slowing in motion and turning into a new direction.

'I think we have arrived,' Adelaide said softly as they both looked out.

The oaks were huge and numerous, the green

leaves of summer upon them and clouds of blue flowers at their feet. A river wound its way alongside the small roadway, more flowers again along the banks. And then after a full five minutes a wider vista opened and a house came into view against the storm-filled sky.

A ruined house, the remains of its walls rent by fire and left roofless and jagged. Thick carved stone sat at its feet, the only part that had not been taken by flame.

So this was Ravenshill. She had heard the stories of its demise back in London, the magnificence it once had been, reduced to a hollow shell that threatened to bankrupt what was left of the Hughes family funds.

The earl had reined in his black steed now and was walking it in a more sedate fashion to one side of the carriage. What was he thinking, she wondered, as he looked at such damage?

When the carriage stopped and the door opened Gabriel Hughes stood hat in hand, his hair only just tethered by a loosened leather tie.

'Welcome to Ravenshill Manor, Adelaide.'

The stark and dramatic truth of the house this

close up was unbelievable, the scent of burning still in the air, but he made no apology for it or explanation.

How had he escaped with his life? was all that she could think. How had anyone managed to get out of this devastation alive?

'If you come with me there is an annex at the back that was not touched. It is a home for now, at least.'

A dozen servants stood in line to one side of the drive, the wind on their faces as they waited.

'If you feel you cannot stay here...'

She stopped him.

'Even as a ruin the place is beautiful.'

For the first time ever he smiled at her without the ghosts of the past in his eyes and the lines that etched each side of his cheeks lessened.

'I always thought so.'

After walking down the row of staff and being presented to each one they made their way around the side of the manor, past the kitchen gardens still surprisingly full of myriad different plants and herbs and into the smaller untouched wing at the back.

It was spartan inside, but the large lobby was open and light.

'We lost much of the furniture and I haven't had the time as yet to replace it.'

The walls were newly painted, she saw as they came into a sitting room, the floors rubbed into shine with a beeswax polish. The furnishings were all of a solid clean line without any excess whatsoever.

A man's room, any small feminine touches completely missing save for a glass vase full of wildflowers that sat on an old desk under the windows.

A pile of books was stacked on another side table, bookmarks of red paper bristling from almost every one. Maps and models of ships completed the tableau. A piano to the far end of the room was surprising.

'Do you play?' she asked and moved towards it. The cover was down and there were initials on the top within a circle of gold and blue.

'Not well.'

GSLH and CEAH. His initials and his sister's, too? She wondered who might have drawn such a thing. A parent, perhaps, the trailing line of darker indigo reaching down into a red heart.

'My grandmother was an artist. The pictures here are all hers.'

Looking around, Adelaide saw that the room held many paintings, of landscapes and houses and in the corner a smaller study framed in gold showed children laughing in the sun.

He caught her glance. 'Charlotte and me, when we were young.'

The two were holding hands, daisies spread about their feet and a large dog beside them.

'The Irish wolfhound's name was Bran. My grandmother enjoyed the exploits of the warrior, Fionn Mac Cunhail. She also thought he would protect us.'

'Protect you from what?' Adelaide's question came unbidden, but there had been something in the tone he used that was not quite right.

'My father was violent sometimes. Bran was trained to growl at noise and one had only to shout to have him bare his teeth in anger.' Unexpectedly he smiled. 'The skeletons in the Wesley family cupboards are numerous and well known.

I am surprised no one has enlightened you on more of our shameful excesses.'

'Scandal being the foremost currency of the *ton*?'

He laughed. 'Well, there is a train of thought that implies it is only other people's misfortunes that make the world go around.'

'Unless its your own world? Then I imagine it would be harder. What happened to your sister?'

'She found her solace in bitterness and my mother's sadness propelled her to flight. A dysfunctional family makes you realise that anything that happens from then on can only be better. There is a certain freedom in that when you are young. It allows you the unfettered opportunity to believe in yourself because nobody else does.'

She touched him then. Simply stepped forward and drew her finger down his cheek. The gold in his eyes was brittle and guarded and he stiffened visibly and tried to move back.

Who else had hurt him? she wondered, as her hand fell to his arm.

'I believe in you, Gabriel.'

He nodded and breathed out shakily, his eyes sliding from contact, but he did not break away from her, either. Rather they stood there in the morning light, two people thrust together in an awkward and unusual marriage.

And right now it had to be enough.

They met later in the afternoon in the kitchen gardens of Ravenshill, more careful of each other after the honesty of their last few meetings.

Gabriel had been out for he had the look of a man new in from exercise, a glow to his cheeks and his jacket over his arm.

'I see that you have taken my advice about walking.'

He laughed. 'You are full of good counsel and the day is a fine one.'

'I had a stroll around the Manor myself. From this direction it looks a little better than at the front.'

He turned to face the structure and breathed out as if even the looking at it was hard. 'Parts of it we may not be able to save, but there are walls that are still structurally sound.'

'Will you rebuild?'

He smiled and the tension seemed to leave the set of his shoulders.

'It will be a long endeavour. I am not certain...'

'We could ask all your friends to come and celebrate starting with a picnic.'

'Here?' From the expression on his face she knew he was not fond of the idea.

'Beginnings are as important as endings, my lord.'

'Gabriel.'

'And the first step is often harder than the last.'

He laughed. 'Little steps. It is what my life has come to these days.'

'You do not think our marriage was a giant leap?'

Again he laughed.

'Let me show you something, Adelaide.'

She followed him down a path behind the house that led through trees and long rows of flowers. A small wooden building sat in a cleared grove.

'Who lives here?'

'I used to.'

'Why?'

'It was a sanctuary.'

Stepping inside, she saw it was bigger than she had thought. A four-poster sat in one corner of the room, heavy brocade curtains hiding it from view. Apart from the bed there were only two chairs placed before the empty grate of a large fireplace.

'I haven't ever brought another person here. You are the first.' The words seemed wrung from him, as if he hadn't wished to say them. 'But then I have not been married before, either.' He smiled.

'Not even close?'

He shook his head. 'Why did you agree to this union, Adelaide? Really?'

A different question from the one she thought he might have asked. 'Perhaps I liked you, too. To talk with.'

The light behind picked up the depths of brown in his hair and the strength of his body, but dulled his features. Like an ancient oil painting etched in shadow.

'Did you ever wonder, Lord Wesley, exactly

where your place was in the world, what your purpose was, and your truth?'

'I did once. Now...' He let the thought linger and frowned. As she waited for an answer he dredged one up. 'Now I am not so certain.'

'The house, you mean, with the fire and the burning?'

He moved back. 'Not so much that, exactly. If it is rebuilt, it is and if it's not, then...'

'You wouldn't care?'

'Less so than I had imagined.'

'At least you have a home, though. Mine was sold when my parents died.'

'So you moved in with your uncle in Sherborne?'

'Not immediately. At first my grandmother took me in, but when she passed away I became wary of...'

'Of life, and of trust.'

He finished the thought for her and she nodded, liking that he understood so clearly. 'Are you?'

'Yes.' He did not stop to give his reply a second thought.

After that there was silence and Adelaide had

the distinct impression that he wished he had not said so much. But something in her had been released by their honesty and she could not let it just stop there.

'Betrayal can have the same sort of effect, I think.' She spoke carefully, gauging his interest. From the sudden stillness she knew he was listening. 'When I was sixteen I was…attacked.'

He turned to face her directly. 'How?'

His concern was warm and real, no hesitation in it or reluctance. If she stepped forward she would be right within his arms. Safe.

'A boy…I knew…tried to…' The words were harder to say than she might have imagined. She had ceased to blame herself for Kenneth Davis's actions years before, but still… 'He tried…to rape me.'

She was against his body before she knew it, close in, his arms about her and his fingers stroking her hair. She could smell sandalwood and leather upon him, his more normal caution replaced by fury.

'Is he still alive?'

'Yes, but his father sent him abroad afterwards and I did not see him again.'

'And your uncle?'

'Never knew.'

Another expletive, this time softer. 'Who did know?'

'My aunts. They said I needed to…forget it… to get over it…to go on…'

'Tell me his name and I will kill him for you.'

At that she laughed because at the time she had desired nothing more than Kenneth Davis's demise in a horrible and slow way.

'I hated him for a good five or so years and then one day I saw that such a loathing was hurting even more than the scratches and bruises and fright he had left me with. So I forgave him, just like that. There is a power in mercy that allows one the will to live again, I think, a force that nullifies the endless wrath. At least it was so with me.'

She could hear his heartbeat through the thin layer of his shirt, the beat slowing to a more even rhythm. His breathing, too, was deeper as long fingers wound into the hair at her nape, the sun rising over the far-off hills bright today and with more than a hint of the warmth to come.

'I would never hurt you, Adelaide. I hope that you at least believe that.'

'I do.'

His awareness of her this time was tempered by anger. She had been hurt and he could help, the shock of betrayal binding them, like iron filings to a magnet, cleaved together by pain.

His wife was a much better person than he was. After the fire both anger and gall had leached the life from his soul and he had not wanted to offer clemency to anyone.

But here, now, for the first time in six months, he felt he was not made of thin glass ready to shatter and splinter under the pressure of emotion or touch.

He had also not thought of his own impotence for all of the last five moments, the ever-consuming sadness and rage diminished by the quiet trust her confession had allowed him.

He wondered then how she would view any sexual intimacy given the horror of her attack.

His celibacy had been forced upon him, but perhaps hers had been, too. He closed his eyes against the measure of terror the sixteen-year-old Adelaide must have felt.

Who had been on her side, hunting out the offender and punishing him? Who had understood her anger and her shame and gone out into the world to diminish it?

Nobody.

She had been as alone as he was with her old unwise aunts and an uncle who seemed to barely know her.

If he ever had a daughter, he would make certain that she knew exactly who to turn to, he promised that he would. The thought caught him unawares and he stiffened.

A daughter.

God.

He had never wanted a wife until now and here he was conjuring up a whole damned family.

An impotent husband does not a father make.

Uncurling his hands, he stepped back, pasting a smile across regret and hoping Adelaide had not seen it.

* * *

He was back to looking furious again, she thought, as he let her go, and her cheeks burnt with the memory of all she had blurted out.

She had not meant to tell anyone, ever, but in the small cottage beside the ruins of his house Gabriel Hughes had looked so damn strong and solid that it had just flowed out, the cork unstopped and years of enforced silence broken.

Making fists of her hands, she tried to find a return to the inconsequential. But it was all so hard.

She liked him.

She did.

She liked every single thing about Gabriel Hughes. His eyes. His body. His voice. His hands. His stillness. His danger. His distance.

He was still hiding things, she knew that, too. She could see it in his eyes and in his stance and in the way he looked at her sometimes as though the truth lay through a gossamer-thin layer of falsity and he wanted her to know it.

But not just yet.

This was their honeymoon and for now they

were skirting around each other, two damaged souls struggling to make sense of things that should never have happened.

Her world had been torn into small chunks of truth that were falling through the air to find a new earthly pattern, locked together before God and the law. Like one of the jigsaws her Aunt Josephine loved, hundreds of pieces, all only waiting to be fitted to form one perfect and complete whole.

Adelaide smiled. She was not perfect and neither was Gabriel Hughes, but together they could be. She at least had to be certain of that. When he turned away to walk out into the sunshine she followed him.

They picked their way towards the Manor, past the ruined walls and blackened timber and then climbing to a higher stand of stone with a platform behind, the pasture studded in clover and daisies.

'This is where I will rebuild at first, out of the wind and with a view across the valley. It will be a smaller house this time, but built on rock.'

'Like the parable in the Bible from Matthew?'

He smiled as though her words held a truth. 'Then the question is, I suppose, am I a wise man or a foolish one?

In answer she simply stamped her feet on the thick bed of stone. The sound travelled around the clearing in an echo.

'It's a beautiful view. Swansdowne, my childhood home, had the same sort of vistas. I remember the river and the trees.' She swept her hand in front of her, indicating the line of oaks along the drive and the lake. 'London holds no real charm against the beauty of the countryside.'

'Amethyst Wylde says the same thing. It's why she seldom ventures down to the city.'

'How did you meet them, the Wyldes, I mean?'

He stooped to pick a sheath of grass and his fingers peeled off the many husks of seed as he spoke. 'Daniel and I were at school together, but it was only later that I got to know him properly. He enjoys horse racing and so did I and we spent a lot of time pitting our skills against each other. He knows horses like the back of his hand.'

'And you?'

'I used to, but it's been a while since I spent a great deal of time upon one.'

'Teach me to ride properly, then, so that I may see the lands of Ravenshill from a horse without being in danger of falling off.'

He was laughing as a shout from behind made him turn. A man whom she did not recognise walked towards them.

'Wesley. I thought it was you.' His smile was wide and generous as Gabriel put out his hand.

'Alexander Watkins, may I introduce you to my new wife, Lady Adelaide Wesley. Alex is a neighbour and an old friend.'

The newcomer smiled. ''Tis a pleasure, my lady. My property borders this one to the east and my own wife will be more than interested to know I have met you. If you would like to visit, we would be more than pleased for the company.' His eyes swept over the vista of the ruined Manor. 'Will you repair it, Gabe?'

'To start with I will build another house up here.'

'A good choice, then. When you begin it I'll give you a hand. I have some cattle you might like to look at, too. A new breeding programme has given me great rewards and…'

Adelaide turned her face into the sun as they were speaking of farming and profit and new breeds of livestock. There could be windows here facing the valley and wide doors to be able to access the lawn and gardens. To plan and build a home was exciting and hopeful, and something she had not thought she would have wanted to do.

She was taken from her reveries by Alexander Watkins saying goodbye and asking them both to come calling on his wife and himself soon.

'Thank you, that would be lovely.' Adelaide was quick to give him a smile as he left.

'I could help him with his eczema.'

'The red and itchy skin on his cheeks?'

'I will make him up a salve and see how he goes with it. I had another patient once at Northbridge with the same complaint, only worse, and I should like to see if it clears up as quickly and completely as hers did.'

Gabriel Hughes stood before her, the light burnishing his face. All the many stories told of him by the *ton* surged into memory: his finesse, his conquests, his name whispered soft in the halls by those who watched him. A lover of great repute who'd left a trail of broken hearts behind him as he passed.

He was married now, though. To her. The ring on the third finger of his left hand caught the sun. She had seen it in the window of Phillips, the jewellers on Bond Street, and had gone in and bought it, a diamond set in the cut of its gold. Bound to each other through life and death, for better or for worse. For richer or for poorer.

He must have seen her worry for he reached out and took her hand, his skin warm from the sun.

A start. A direction.

She wished he might kiss her, hard and slow and well. But he did not. Rather he tucked her arm into his and led her back to the annex behind the Manor.

Chapter Fifteen

An hour after supper he knocked at the door of the chamber Adelaide was using and waited until she came to open it. She had let her hair down, he saw, and the chestnut of it curled to her waist.

'I thought we might talk.' He smiled, the edges of his eyes creasing in humour.

'Here?' Uncertainty lay in her query.

'It's private.' His glance went to a book left open on the small table near the chair. When she hurried over to close it he caught sight of small neat rows of writing.

A diary and full of the worry he could see so plainly on her face? Once he had written his thoughts and dreams down, too. God, that seemed like for ever ago.

'It is poetry. I am certain that they are dreadful and I have never shown another soul, but…I write them anyway, sometimes two or three a day and then not for months.'

'But today the muse struck?'

'With a vengeance. I imagine I shall burn them all before the week's end, but for now they help.'

'Help make sense of what is between us?'

Her smile dulled. 'Or of what is not, my lord?'

She was braver than any woman he had ever met and much more direct. Under the valour he saw other things, too, fright and concern the most noticeable amongst them. He should tell her all that he was and was not but even the thought made him blanch.

'I had imagined…' She stopped and then began again. 'I had imagined it different…the intimacy of a marriage.'

'What was it you had envisaged?'

The corners of her mouth turned in a smile.

'This,' she answered, bringing her arms around his neck. 'And this,' she added, touching her lips to his before pressing down, the magic of him exploding into every part of her.

She had no idea quite what happened next given her lack of any experience, but she had read numerous romance books from the library and could guess at some of the ramifications of what she was doing.

But he surprised her as he dragged her forward, slanting her mouth to his own and tasting. No restraint in it, either, though there was anger, too, amidst the need as his fingers threaded through her hair. Their breath combined in the closeness and his heart beat like a drum, pounding between them with such a force that she pulled back.

'Adelaide.' Her name before his mouth returned, his tongue forcing itself in and then she was falling and falling outside of herself and deep into the ache of promise and hope. No boundaries, no notion of where he stopped and she began, a mutual sharing at the well of wonder. Nothing mattered save them here, pressed against each other and asking for whatever they would give, or take. Just lust, the roiling truth of it in the way he deepened the kiss, brokering no refusal and accepting no passive response.

She let him in without holding anything back; he was strong and beautiful, enigmatic and dangerous. All those flavours and more, the sadness in him and the anger were a part of what he showed her, too, as he let her understand just what one could know from a kiss.

And when she thought she might begin to comprehend, he held her still, the shaky sound of her own breath filling the room as he broke the contact.

'I am sorry.' He whispered this as she closed her eyes, the red warm world of sensation lessening, blurred by disbelief.

I am sorry? Sorry because he could not utter the words she might have liked to hear, the forever words, the loving words? Sorry because she could feel the tremble of unease that ran through him as easily as if it were her own?

Adelaide's nails dug into his arms and he knew she wanted more. His heart pounded as noticeably as it always did when he touched her, but his member had not risen. Nay, it lay warm in the crease of his groin, a quiet thing of no mind for all he'd felt as he kissed her.

The anger in him seethed, and the shame, the manners he usually held on to squeezing through the fury. He needed to be away from such failure, to ride against the wind and the rain and the open air until the roiling unfairness of what had happened to him settled and he could cope again.

But he didn't dare to leave her here, alone with her quick mind to pull all the pieces together and make a sense of them. He wanted neither pity nor help. He didn't wish for mesmerising or sympathy, either, hapless words against a condition that was unchangeable.

His mind wanted her, God, it did without a doubt, but his body and flesh had not made the connection. Would they ever?

Tonight she had initiated the play with the flush of sex on her cheeks and the look of wonder in her eyes, as beguiling as hell and as sensual. Six months ago he would have been on her, emptying his seed until well into the night, a shared pleasure, a mutual satisfaction. But he was dead now from the waist down, withered and perished and numb.

Gabriel Hughes. Impotent.

How people would laugh should that come to be known.

By anyone at all.

He set her back from him, making sure that she could stand and was glad that she looked away. He could not answer questions or feign humour. He could barely even manage to speak.

'I shall see you tomorrow, sweetheart.' The endearment rolled off his tongue unmindful and he bowed slightly before leaving the room.

Sweetheart? Was she truly that? Adelaide breathed out. Hard.

If so, why did he not stay to take his ease, and lie beside her? Could he not see that she wanted him to? Should she simply say it to him? *Stay with me. Hold me. Show me what it is to love a woman well.*

Her only experience at a sexual intimacy had been Kenneth Davis's brutal attack on her all those years ago and in the darkness and terror she had no real idea as to what had happened to his body. Gabriel was soft and slow and burning, his hands against her skin as if they wanted to be there, as if she were precious and beautiful and needed.

She still felt the shock of his mouth and the silver flame of light that rose to envelop her, his breath and her breath one, and an age-old knowledge of each other that needed no formal tuition.

She felt quickened somehow, waiting for more, a need that had no beginning or end, but just was.

Her aunts could have told her what this all meant had they still been alive, with all their reading and far-ranging knowledge, but there was no one else to ask. No sisters or cousins. No friends whom she might have confided in, either.

Alone.

She had always been that. Even at Northbridge in the care of her uncle, her fear of venturing out further after Kenneth Davis's attack growing through the years, rather than diminishing. The village girls treated her with respect and her patients with more, but she had never had true friendship until now with Gabriel Hughes. She had told him her deepest secret and enjoyed every single conversation and she had married him for ever.

Before she knew what she was doing she had a thick shawl around her shoulders and, taking a candle, opened the door and followed him.

Gabriel was tired of it all.

He wanted to enjoy his wife in the deepest sense of doing so, with his whole body and his mind. Tonight had left him tense and wound up as tight as any spring. He ached to know how far Adelaide might let him go and if his body naked against her own would respond in the way he had long since forgotten.

'God, please help me.' He whispered this into the smallness of his chamber and crossed to the window.

It was warm and he took off his cravat and un-buttoned his shirt.

He saw her reflection in the glass as she stood behind him, the pale of her face and the candle flickering. He brought the folds of linen together so that at least his chest was not bare. Then he turned.

'Adelaide.'

'Gabriel.' She seldom said his name unbidden and he liked the sound of it from her lips, almost bold.

'I want to be married…properly. I want you to take me to your bed and help me to understand what it means to be a wife.'

No hidden meanings, no unexplained intentions. So like her to place things down like that. The danger intensified. But she was beside him now and parting the front of his shirt before reaching in.

He waited, feeling the familiar instant spark, but nothing more. Still, the smell of her close and the soft curl of her hair held him captive and when she looked up it was easy to bring her into his arms.

He could pleasure her. He could still do that. A new excitement clung to defeat. His body was not useless. It was well practised and most efficient at eliciting what a woman desired.

Second nature. Understood. An authority and a master at the gentle arts of loving. Even if finally it was not enough, he knew he would try.

'Are you sure?'

She smiled and that was what did it, the happiness in her and the humour. He had never taken a woman to bed he truly liked... That truth left him astonished, but he shook it away and lifted her into his arms.

This time he was careful, careful as he sat her down on his bed and slipped off her shoes, careful as he undid the ties of her bodice so that each loosened thread exposed the soft fabric of a chemise beneath.

He had always relied on sex as a means of communication but here now it was the loving that he could give her. A different approach, softer, quieter, the feel of her skin, the rise of her flesh.

One hand slipped inside the shell of lawn over her breast, feeling, exploring, his thumb against her nipple, moving quickly and then quicker again. She stiffened and arched and then stayed still, the bud he caressed proud and hard.

Then the fabric lay pooled about her waist, the wide skirt of her gown beneath it, the candles on the mantel throwing her breasts into a mix of shadow and light.

So very beautiful.

And his.

Dipping his head, he used his tongue, trailing a pathway along the side of her throat on to the collarbone and down to the plumpness before covering her nipple, his hands cupping the round and bringing her closer, the sweet taste in him as he shut his eyes.

Always before he had been mindful. Of the armoire nearby. Of the small room off a bed-chamber. Of the dangers and secrets of a house waiting to be discovered.

But here, now, he thought of nothing save Adelaide, of her grace and her humour, of her bravery and acquiescence, of the way she made small noises to show him that what he did was beautiful and that she was grateful for it.

A rush of sadness surprised him, the poignancy of all he had missed and all he had ruined there in that one moment of mindfulness, and then another thought that had him reeling.

He loved her.

He loved his wife.

He loved Adelaide beyond reason and comprehension and he had done so since the first moment of meeting her.

She was his for always, with her wit and her wisdom, with her smiles and her goodness and truth.

He couldn't remember ever feeling as if he was not the one in charge, he who had always easily been able to translate the needs of the feminine sex and give them exactly what they wanted.

But now the rules seemed to have changed and instead of distance he was completely involved. Her skin against his own, the touch of flesh, her breath warm where his shirt fell open to bareness. The way her hair tickled his arms as it fell long and dark almost to her waist.

She smelt of lemon, clean and fresh, the heavier perfumes of the *ton* washed away by lightness. He smiled into the scent, wanting it to fill him up with all of the things he hadn't had much pleasure of in the capturing of secrets.

Shaking his head, he laid his mouth against the beating vein in her throat. He had killed people by pressing down on such a spot and hardly a backward glance, another job, a further instruction.

He had not told Adelaide all of it, but sometimes in the heart of lust there also lay the spectre of death—husbands who would betray a nation, brothers with treason in their eyes.

He'd never made love before and been able to relax like this, never had the luxury of time and safety. His glance fell to the scars on his hand, disfigured against the beauty of her.

He would never be perfect, but he could not let Adelaide go. Rising, he caught her chin and covered her mouth with a groan of both ownership and surrender.

This kiss was different, Adelaide thought, intense and deeper, like words that he could not as yet say.

Oh, but how she wanted him, closer, naked, lying with her on a bed of moonlight and showing her exactly what it was she needed.

'Gabriel?'

He glanced up, eyes unguarded, pools of gold and the ends of tawny-and-red curls falling

across his face. In London she had thought he
looked like a hardened angel, but tonight she
could easily see the vulnerability and the sadness clinging to a ragged edge of hope.

'I want you,' she said, then as his hands found
the hem of her dress and rose upward she forgot
to think at all.

She woke alone, in her own room in her own
bed, a sprig of lavender lying across the pillow.
She was naked, she knew that even as her fingers
went to the place that her husband's had been,
the secret warmth beating and a wetness there
she had not known before.

No wonder Gabriel Hughes's name was whispered in the way that she had heard it, with rev-
erence and intrigue and plain pure want.

I want you.

She remembered moaning his name again and
again as he had taken her to the stars and the
moon and the heavens with his clever fingers and
his soothing mouth. And after he had placed one
hand across her stomach and another behind her.

'Can you feel that?' When he had pressed down

the echoes of what had been became stronger, the heel of his hand low and deep. 'With touch a climax can be extended. Claim it, Adelaide, for me.'

And she had, rising against his palm and arching as ecstasy beached across her, deeper this time and longer, wringing the life from any pride she still had left, the sensation of heat and release making her float until her body was nothing but feeling and vibration.

My God, she had barely recognised the woman she had become. He could have done anything at all to her and she would have welcomed it, her, the paragon of spinsterhood and common sense and good manners.

Turning into the pillow, she hid her face, wondering about the smile that tugged at her lips and made her giggle.

Gabriel Hughes, the fourth Earl of Wesley, was hers for ever. Nights of lust under moonlight for the rest of her life. And yet worry blossomed beneath the realisation. What of him? How had he found his pleasure in what they had done? She had barely touched him and he had not wanted her to, either. She remembered running her hand up his inner thigh, but he had captured her fingers and laid them instead upon her breast, wetting them with his mouth so that the heat and the cold made her shiver and then understand.

In the opposites one could find fulfilment. He had been gentle and then rough as his teeth had come where her fingers rested, and the edge of pain had also become the edge of pleasure.

She stilled in order to concentrate on the throb that began to beat with just her thoughts. She wanted him again and again, here and now, in the sunlight and the morning, her legs splayed apart as her fingers sought the flesh swollen from his touch.

Desperate. Had he made her that? With his expertise and his learning. There were no tears at such a thought, but only the beating, dancing delight of anticipation and desire.

Adelaide heard voices as she came down the stairs an hour later and her hands fisted at her sides. In this state of mind she had no want to deal with strangers, though as she listened more carefully she realised it was Lord and Lady Montcliffe.

Would they know? Could they tell? Was there some understanding between married people that she had not known of before, some secret club, some untold confidence? She had hidden the marks Gabriel had left upon her body under a swathe of lace about her neck, but she knew in her eyes and on her face there would be glimmers of all she remembered. She could not even look at her husband as she came into the room, but smiled as Amethyst Wylde took her hand.

'I hope you don't mind our intrusion, Adelaide. Daniel had to come this way to see about a horse and so we chanced it and dropped in for he had some news to share with Gabriel.'

'I am glad you came for it is lovely to see you.' And it was, she thought, for these people were interesting and generous and warm. She included Daniel Wylde in the comment as they sat down again, glad when the men left Amethyst and her to converse alone.

'Christine Howard said I was to give you her

love and to say that the lotion you made for her mother seems to be doing the trick.'

'I suppose I should have made some up for Gabriel's mother, too, for she seems most unhappy.'

'Oh, that will be all due to his sister's problems. I have only met Charlotte Hughes briefly and she was a beautiful but bitter woman. It seems the man she had met in Edinburgh was already married according to Lucien's mother and so she is coming back to London.'

Adelaide was glad she was not venturing north to Ravenshill Manor instead. She wanted a few weeks to understand what marriage was about without others staying in the small annex with Gabriel and her.

'Is this the news you said that Daniel brought with him?'

'No. it was something else entirely.' By the brief flare in her eyes Adelaide knew Amethyst did not wish to divulge the matter.

Daniel had also asked her something from the other side of the room and, looking over at him, her eyes collided with pale gold, the humour in them so at odds with the complete embarrassment in her own.

'I'm sorry...?'

Lord Wylde repeated his words.

'I was thinking that married life appears to agree with you, Adelaide, and with Gabriel.'

He was teasing, she knew, but a wash of red covered her face before she could stop it and for one moment she even thought she might burst into tears. My God, what was happening to her? She had always been able to cope with conversations and challenges and yet here she was after one wondrous night unable to find her equilibrium.

Gabriel saved her by standing and drawing attention back to himself. 'Daniel is here to look at a horse at Colton House. I'd heard about the stud, but I have not been up there.'

'Come with us, then. I would value your opinion of the animal, Gabe. We need not be long.'

'Would you like that, Adelaide?' Her husband's full glance was upon her now but it was gentle, giving her the choice of whether they went or not.

'I would. Is Colton far?'

'No. Only forty or so minutes away. There is a tavern nearby, too, that has an excellent luncheon.'

Amethyst looked more than pleased. 'We'll have a short walk together whilst the men look over the livestock. The day is beautiful after all and I have a need for exercise after the carriage ride for my back is hurting me.'

Daniel looked a little concerned. 'The doctor said you were not to overdo things, Amethyst...'

Lady Montcliffe laughed. 'Wait until you are pregnant, Adelaide. My husband has turned into a fussy mother hen who would like to wrap me in cotton wool and keep me from doing anything. Do not worry, my dearest. This child is at least a month away yet. We women know these things.' Her hands lay on the bulge beneath her skirts and her voice was warm—a beautiful Madonna who understood the power of her imminent motherhood very well.

Adelaide chanced a glance at Gabriel and was astonished at the look that lay so visibly in his eyes. Regret. Longing. Or just plain uncertainty. She could not quite decide.

Chapter Sixteen

The stud farm was large but well laid out and as the men went to the stables with the lord of the house, the two women struck out down a pathway overshadowed by weeping willow trees, the lime-green colour of their leaves in the light astonishing.

'I'd heard the gardens here were beautiful, but I did not expect them to be so marvellous,' Amethyst said. 'Lord Herbert has no wife so it must be he who professes an interest in plantings as well as horseflesh.' She laughed. 'He seemed a good man. Perhaps Christine Howard might come with us next time.'

'If you are matchmaking, it seldom works, I hear.' Adelaide gave this advice with a smile.

'Well, do not be certain about that. Papa was

the one who chose Daniel for me and that has been most satisfactory. My father was ill, you see, and thought he had not long to live.'

The next quarter of an hour was spent on the story behind such a statement and Adelaide was delighted by Amethyst's honesty. She had heard a little of it whilst in London, but the truth of what had transpired was both funny and poignant.

'So your father is still managing with his heart complaint?'

'Brilliantly. He seldom is in bed and his new wife, bless her, is the sort who refuses to believe he is sick anyway. As his desire is to have as many grandchildren as he has the luck to meet I am doing my best to make his wishes come true.'

'Your other child is only young, isn't she?'

'Sapphire is almost ten months old. She is a beautiful little girl who—'

Amethyst suddenly clutched her side and paled considerably, breathing out with quiet deliberation as she bent over. A stab of worry had Adelaide taking her hand; the pulse at her wrist was racing and she felt clammy though the fingers wrapped tightly about her own.

'Are you all right?' Adelaide knew that she wasn't even as she asked the question.

'I need to…sit…down.' Her voice was breathless and shallow, a gust of wind making her teeth chatter as she collapsed against a small bank.

There was only grass and dirt to sit on and Amethyst Wylde had begun to shake quite badly. From fear and shock, Adelaide thought, her own mind turning over possibilities as to what was wrong and what might happen next.

The gush of water gave her that answer and Amethyst began to cry. 'I can't have the baby now… I need Daniel…' She stopped speaking as the first contraction came, concentrating on the new pains that racked her.

Oh, my God, Adelaide thought. *She will have the baby here and I am the only one around to help in the delivery.* Her mind could not quite believe what was happening, but she had enough sense not to panic. One of them had to remain calm if this was going to turn out as she hoped and they were too far away from the house for anyone to hear her even if she did cry for help.

No, it was up to her. She was all there was. Without hesitation she stripped off her wide skirt and tucked it about Amethyst's shoulders as both a blanket and a cushion. Amethyst Wylde needed warmth and she needed reassurance and she, Adelaide Ashfield, was damned well going to give it to her. Adelaide Wesley, she amended as she removed her petticoats. She would need cloth to wipe down the baby and to wrap it. The soft, clean lawn was exactly right.

Unexpectedly Amethyst smiled as she saw what was happening.

'I…am…sorry…Adelaide.' Her teeth clattered together as she spoke. 'If you want to leave me and get someone else…'

'There is no time and besides I am more than capable of delivering this baby. You have absolutely nothing to worry about.'

Fright warred with strength inside her but, even though she had never attended a birth, her aunts had always had much to say on the subject. Lifting up Amethyst's skirts, she placed her hands on the taut belly.

'This is Nature working at its most efficient, you see, and babies that come quickly are usually delivered with ease. Was your first birth quick, too?'

'Yes. It was f-f-fast and furious.' Cold hands tightened across her own. 'Please stay with me, Adelaide. I could not do it alone and I am scared.'

'Of course I am going nowhere. And look, the sun is out. Your baby will be born into a grotto of green and yellow. I think that is a sign of well-being and harmony and just think of the story you will be able to tell your papa.'

Things happened both quickly and slowly after that. Adelaide had no true sense of time as the contractions came closer together and then suddenly the child was in her hands, his eyes opening, a breath and then a lusty cry.

'A little boy,' she told Amethyst, who was trying to raise herself on her elbows to see. 'And he is perfect.'

After checking his mouth and nose and wrapping the baby in the lawn she placed him on

Amethyst's chest, making sure the cord was not ruptured and then beginning to massage her stomach.

Five moments later the placenta was delivered and the bleeding stopped completely. For the first time in over an hour Adelaide took a breath that was normal and looked over at her charges.

Both looked peaceful now, the dappled light across them, the tiny hands of the infant pummelling against its mother's flesh as he suckled, dark hair at his nape still wet from birth.

My God, she had done it. She had brought a child into the world and helped his mother. A joy she had not felt before rushed through her as she wiped her hands against the fabric in her bodice and pushed back her loosened hair.

Gabriel found his wife with her hair down, her skirts missing and blood across her face and hands. But it was Daniel's cry that truly alerted him to what had happened as he crouched near his wife and lifted her up to him.

A baby. A birth.

'Adelaide helped me. She did…everything.'

Amethyst Wylde had burst straight into tears and was now clinging to her husband. The servant behind was dispatched to the house to bring a dray and quickly.

'I am certain they will both be fine.' Adelaide stood up from where she had sat and Gabriel's arm went to steady her. 'The baby cried immediately and then began to feed, so although it is early I do not think there will be a problem.'

Taking his jacket off, Gabriel laid it around his wife's shoulders, buttoning the garment to the neck. A thin undershift was all that she had on from her waist down and she was shaking violently.

When he had first come into the clearing he thought Adelaide had been hurt badly with the amount of blood around her and the position she sat in, strains of Henrietta Clements coming back and all the death and blood of the Service. He had felt his heart simply stop, the frozen waste of clogging breath. And then the baby had cried.

If he should ever lose Adelaide... If she should die...

His arms tightened across her shoulders as he held her to him.

'I'd never done it before, though I told Amethyst that I had.' She whispered this so that the others would not hear and the earnestness of her confession was heartbreaking.

His wife had not thought to run for help or gone to pieces. No, she had stripped off her own clothes and coped with it all. Even in terror and inexperience, even without the absolute rudiments of anything to help her.

'If one…panics it always…goes wrong, Aunt… Jean said. She said one has to keep…a composure and a peacefulness for the event otherwise a child might be…difficult to deliver…' The trembling had worsened and without thought he lifted her up to him and took her over to a tree where he sat down with it at his back and with her in his lap, trying to give her the warmth and reassurance she needed.

Now that help had arrived she was panicking. In fact, she thoroughly went to pieces in his arms, her sobs ragged and deep, his warrior of the healing arts finally reaching the limit of what could be tolerated.

'It's all right, sweetheart. Everything is all right now.'

And it was, he realised with a great thump of truth. His wife was in his arms and the world was still going around. That was all he needed. Just Adelaide and her bravery and strength. Just them. Together.

Much later they returned to Ravenshill Manor, Amethyst and Daniel electing to stay on at Colton House with their newly born son and a doctor who had been summoned by Lord Herbert.

Adelaide was exhausted. Gabriel had given her the choice of staying or making for home, but it seemed all she could think of was being somewhere safe, and the annex at the rear of the Manor was where she felt the most secure.

Gabriel dismissed the astonished Milly when they came into her room, telling her he wanted to help his wife himself.

And he did help her, rolling off her stockings and undressing her with an extreme tenderness, and then finding a cloth and ewer to dab at her hands and face.

Finally he placed her into bed, the clean sheets against her skin.

'Please…come in with me…I am…fr-freezing.'

He hesitated momentarily, but then, stripping off his jacket and pants, he joined her. He left on the long linen shirt and held her close, pulling the blankets around her chin.

'Thank God you were with Amethyst…'

But she simply stopped him with her own words.

'No, Gabriel. Thank God I am with you.'

Then she fell promptly asleep.

An amazing statement when he considered her day, but here after cold and shock and in desperate tiredness he believed her.

He had never had someone true and good on his side before, not like this. Her ring glinted in the light of a single ten-hour candle, but when he laid his warm hand on top of hers it curled about his own, even in sleep.

Safe. She felt safe here at Ravenshill with him in the small annex at the back of the ruined manor. She had not wished to stay at Colton House with all its splendour and luxury, but had elected to return to the place she felt at home in.

His wife.

His saviour.

Usually at this time of night he was prowling the dark watches and the shadows, aware that sleep was very far away and waiting for the dawn.

But here at barely nine o'clock in the evening he was anchored to this bed and wrapped in the long limbs of Adelaide, tethered by something far more enduring than anger, sorrow and shame.

Shutting his eyes, Gabriel said a prayer. For them, for the baby that had been born, for the years he might have with his wife and for the joy that would follow.

And it was only as he fell into slumber Gabriel realised he had not asked God for the miracle of a healing for himself. In fact, he had forgotten about it altogether.

He came awake in the night, the warmth of Adelaide beside him, her hand across his stomach and her leg slung over his thighs. And in the quiet he reached down into her centre as a moth flies to flame, gentle and soft, her body writhing with the touch.

Up into warmth and wetness and the hidden depths of life, he turned her as she opened her thighs and took her across him, almost real, the bud of her arousal harnessed against his thumb as he quickened his rhythm.

He felt her come, the beaching waves of release, rigid and then loose and quiet. When he pressed in again straight afterwards she cried out, but he covered her mouth with his own and brought her to the flurry of a second climax, this one clenching hard over him and making her shake with the intensity of it.

Like birth, he thought.

Like the beginning.

Lifting his fingers to his mouth, he tasted her sweetness.

She was lost in love, shivering now with delight instead of fear as she reached all the places he wanted to show her and then held her whilst she recovered.

The candle burned low and the moon had waned, the dawn not far off, she thought, for already the eastern sky had lightened through the crack in the curtains. She cuddled in, her hand inadvertently touching the twisted skin at his thigh as she did so.

When he stiffened she knew why he had left his shirt on. He didn't want her to see this or to know it. When his hand came down over hers though she simply pushed him away and continued to explore through touch. A burn, she surmised, for nothing else could have left a mark quite like this one. The fire in the chapel at Ravenshill.

'Did it hurt?'

She felt him smile into her hair.

'Yes.'

'Who tended you?'

'The Wesley physician.'

'Did he use honey?'

'I don't think so.'

'Lavender oil, then, or diluted vinegar?'

He shook his head. 'He wrapped the leg in wet bandages and changed them frequently for a very long time.'

'And is the pain still there?'

'Sometimes.'

'I will make you something for it, then, to relax the tightness. Is it on your stomach as well?'

She went to reach up further, but he stopped her by capturing her palm and bringing it to his lips where he kissed each finger.

'Clever hands. Healing hands, hands that have brought a child who was not meant to have arrived so soon safely into this world. Daniel will never be able to thank you enough. I think he will be your servant for life.'

She giggled, imagining the lofty and austere Lord Montcliffe in such a role. 'I would rather his friendship.

'Well, I am sure that you will have that.'

She liked the laughter in his words and the way his fingers traced circles across the bare skin on her back.

'Would you like to have children, Gabriel?'

All movement stopped and his breathing became shallow.

'Our children, I mean,' she added as he did not say anything. 'An heir for the Wesley title and lands?'

She made herself carry on. 'I do not know a lot about what happens between a man and a woman in bed, but I do imagine it is something like the farmyard and there has to be a contact between us that is...more intimate.'

He still did not answer though his heart raced hard in his chest. She could feel it through the linen.

'If you would like to do this thing, I would be happy to do it with you.'

His swear word took her by surprise as he rolled away from their embrace and sat up on the bed. His profile against the new dawn looked wary and tired, a man fighting more demons than he might ever name.

'Is it some illness that stops you?'

He stood at that and pulled down his shirt, reaching for the candle and blowing it out. The smoke curled into the grey light, a small puff of blackness and then gone.

Like her husband.

Without another word he had disappeared through the door frame and shut it behind him.

She did not see Gabriel until well into the next day when she spied him on horseback on one of the hills a good distance from the house. She knew him from the easy style he had of riding, fluid and graceful, and because the horse was the same one that he had ridden beside the carriage on the journey up from London.

Walking purposefully down to the stables, she thought to intercept him and indeed as she came down the pathway he was cantering in from the other direction, a groom coming to take the steed into the stables proper.

And leaving them to face each other.

'You ride well.' It was the only thing she could even think to say that did not include a question.

He smiled and hit his whip against his jodhpurs, a cloud of dust rising as he did so.

'Practice makes perfect.'

She was at a loss as to how to reply. He had had a lot of practice in the bedroom and yet…

It was as though he could see what she was thinking. 'We need to talk, Adelaide, but not here. If you could meet me in the blue salon in, say…an hour?'

He sounded so serious her heart began to beat quicker, a new dread coming from nowhere. Would he tell her that this marriage was a mistake or that he never wanted children? A hundred other possibilities crossed her mind, all fleeing as he stepped forward and placed one warm hand across hers.

'It is my problem, Adelaide. Not yours.' And with that he walked back into the stable to see about his horse.

He watched the clock on the wall slow in its minutes as it turned towards eleven. He had to be honest with her, he had to tell her who he was now, a man ruined from circumstance and foolishness, a broken man who should never have married her.

'God, help me.' The words echoed in the room

and in his stomach, hollow and sick, scared and lonely. This was the truth of him. This man.

He swore again beneath his breath when he heard her coming, light footsteps on the parquet floor. Could he do it? Would he do it? How was one to sacrifice heaven for hell and barely a backward glance?

'Thank you for coming.' She was here now and he crossed to close the door behind her, standing against it for a moment in indecision, weighing up his strength.

'You thought I would not?' The nervously asked question helped somewhat as did the shake in her fingers as she wiped back a curl that had fallen across her cheek.

He wanted to step forward and hold her, make her understand all that he was inside even amongst the shattered fragments. But it was not fair to do so. He had to give her the facts to make her own decision about their marriage without coercion. Without feeling. Cold. Hard. Honest.

I am impotent.

Say it, his body chided, but his mind refused. He hated the way he was breathing fast and the sickness was again back, sweeping over him so that he could barely take in air.

He sat down hard on the chair behind him and held his head spinning with the horror of everything. For one moment he thought he might even cry in front of her like a baby.

And then she was beside him, her hand across his brow and at his wrist, feeling for the signs of sickness, he thought, trying to determine what to do.

Fix me up. Make me better. Make me the man I once was with your potions and your kindness. Make me whole again.

These words turned in his mind. Foolish hopes that would never come to pass.

'I might be able to help you, Gabriel, if you could only tell me what's wrong.'

He shook his head. 'No one can help me.' He hated the self-pity he could hear in his words, but could not take them back.

And then because she had seen him at his very worst, a man with nothing left to lose save his final pride, he simply blurted it out.

'I cannot make love any more because I am

impotent. The accident took that part from me, the burns, the fire. I cannot father children. I cannot be a husband. I should have told you, of course I should have before you married me, but I wanted...'

He stopped and swallowed. 'I love you, Adelaide, and I wanted you to love me back.'

Adelaide could not believe the words he said. Not the ones on impotency and the fire and burns, but the other ones; the ones of love and wanting.

'I love you, too, Gabriel. With all my heart and soul. I loved you from the first moment of meeting you, the very first in the small arbour at the Bradford ball when you warned me about your reputation.'

Placing her hands on either side of his face, she knelt down beside him and looked into his eyes, a darker bruised gold today, though a flare of hope was there, too, amongst the anguish and disbelief.

'The physical things you speak of are only one side of a union. What of trust and love and closeness? A marriage is about friendship and honesty and laughter. I have all of that with you. And more...' She smiled. 'When you take me to bed I cannot remember anything at all save the way you make me feel. If that is our life, then I am more than happy with it, though I should like to be able to pleasure you, too. You could teach me.'

He stood at that and brought her into his arms, the scent of soap and linen filling in the cold of the room. He had washed and shaved since she had seen him last, the hair at his nape still damp, spots of water darkening the loosely tied cravat he wore at his neck.

Beautiful. More beautiful than she had ever seen him with the edge of vulnerability staining his eyes and deepening the lines in his cheeks.

Not a boy but a man, honed by tragedy, seasoned by fire.

'And the promise of children, Adelaide? What of this loss?'

'We shall enjoy the offspring of your friends. Already there are two little Wyldes whom we can shower with our love. Your friends will have others.'

She felt him smile rather than saw it, felt him relax and meld into the shape of her, exhausted by his truths.

'I don't deserve you.'

'Why?'

'Because you did not know who I once was and that is unfair. All you have now is the wreck of me.'

'And what of me, Gabriel? Did you know the girl who used to laugh more, enjoy life more? The one who was not scared of strangers and men and the midnight dark? That girl was lost, too, with Kenneth Davis's attack, gone in a second, replaced by a new woman. But you know me as I am now, lessened, less trusting, more uncertain. I hope it is enough.'

'Enough?'

'Marriage is just that, don't you think? Change and challenge and chance. The people we are now will be different from the ones we will be in ten years or twenty. Or fifty when we are old and grey and wrinkled. But will we love each other less because of life marking us, moulding us, strengthening us? Like steel in a forge, stron-

ger in adversity and more tempered. Less break-
able because of the hardships and of the joy.'

'I love you, sweetheart. I love you so much
that it hurts, here.' He placed one of her hands
across his heart and she could feel the thump of
it, neither as fast as it had been, nor as heavy. She
was glad for the fact even as sadness crouched
close, for him and for her and for the things they
would not have together, but also for all he had
just given her. Love. Truth. Himself.

And then just like that his touch changed back
into the magic, drawing a line down her neck
and on to the flesh above her bodice in the way
only he was able to.

'You are so beautiful,' he whispered, his lips
grazing the place where his fingers had been,
down and down on to the rise of her breast. She
felt his tongue there, too, the dampness and the
heat, and then a heavy suckling, hollowed and
echoing. Sounds of her heartbeat and her breath
and then his and an answering call somewhere
lower. *Take me*, it cried, *and make me yours*. And
he did then, with his hands and a swift sharp-
ness that had her arching backwards, the heavy

beat of blood and want coursing through her. Her fingers were now in his hair, pulling him in, making him hers.

'I love you.' Softly said and formless. He took her loving and stretched it around desire and appetite before changing it again to the white-hot heat of knowledge.

When he was finished and she simply stood there watching him, spent, he took her hand and laid it across his nipple.

'Here,' he instructed, 'like this,' he added, shepherding her fingers and pinching in a certain spot between forefinger and thumb.

She understood what he was doing. In the ashes of honesty a new phoenix was rising, a different one, a finer one. Together they could make this marriage the best it could be. She licked the tips of her fingers as he had done with her and set to work.

When the bud hardened she was pleased and when his breathing ran into quickness she was even more so.

And then she laid her mouth on his and found the taste of him with her tongue, slanting across wetness, taking the breath from them both, the power he allowed her now more exciting than anything she had ever known.

This was what it was like to truly love someone without reservation or embarrassment. Threading her fingers around his neck, she brought him down with her on to the thick burgundy rug.

'I will never stop loving you, Gabriel. Ever.'

'And I will make certain that you do not,' he whispered back.

They barely left Gabriel's bedchamber the next day and the one after that as they discovered things about each other by talking through the hours.

'I think Henrietta Clements meant to take me with her when she died because I did not love her enough.' It was late afternoon and they were sitting near the window, wrapped in each other's arms in the large leather wingchair.

'Was it she who set the fire, do you think?' Adelaide's question came quietly and just like that the last piece of the puzzle clicked into place.

The candle. The flame. The chapel curtain dust-dry with age.

'Yes,' he said, the last vestige of doubt falling away. 'It was she. I remember now.'

He'd gone to meet her because she had sent him a message. She had the names of those her husband was associating with, the men and women who might bring down a kingdom at worst or a government at best.

He had not wanted to go, he knew that, because already there was a glint of madness in her eyes that worried him.

She had pulled a gun on him as he arrived and made him stand still, there by the marbled font, under the ruined body of Christ. Her hands had been shaking so much he thought the weapon might have gone off without her even meaning to shoot him.

'Place your right hand on the Bible, Gabriel.'

He had done so, waiting for his chance to disarm her.

'Swear you will love me for ever, in God's name. I want to hear you say it now and mean it.'

He'd swallowed and hesitated. He wasn't a

man unable to use a lie for his own means even in a house of God, but there was something else at play here, something hidden and desperate.

'Say it.'

As one hand had covered her belly in that certain protective gesture he suddenly understood.

'You are with child?'

She had nodded, the gun lowering, but not forgotten.

'Is it mine?'

Please, God, let it not be. If you ever do anything at all for me, my lord, please do not let this child be mine.

She shook her head and relief flooded through him. 'But it's not my husband's, either. George Friar, my husband's cousin, took me against my will and I could not stop him.'

She was crying. Loudly. 'I think he would kill Randolph if he had the chance, too. Take me away with you, Gabriel, because you are the only one who has ever been truly kind to me. Say you love me and we can be free.'

And when he could not the candle was in her

hand and then it was within the old curtain dividing the font from the chapel proper.

The horror must have shown on his face as the flame took, for she suddenly and simply stepped back into it, fire racing up her wide skirts and into her loosened hair.

He had tried to save her, tried to find the woman under the heat and bring her out, but the smoke had billowed, death tracing their skin with its blackness, the last echo of reason as he reached for the water in the font and poured it across them.

'It was a month before I remembered anything again,' he said softly as Adelaide's hands traced the ravages of fire upon his thigh. 'For a time I thought it was me who had killed her and then bits came back.' Guilt made his voice hoarse. 'We both betrayed each other, I think, her in love and me for the love of secrets. She was a means to an end and I deserved all that I have now.' He sat up straighter and frowned. 'But she gave me the names and I remember them now. George Friar is the one who killed Randolph Clements, the one we want.'

'We?'

'The Service. When Daniel was here he brought me a letter from Alan Wolfe that said Henrietta's husband had been murdered. They found his body in a tavern near Oxford. Odds are it was Friar's work for he has left his lodgings and disappeared.'

'To go where?'

'That's what I plan to find out.'

'I met him at an afternoon soirée in London just before we were married and he insinuated he knew about Kenneth Davis and the way he had attacked me. He wanted me to go with him as his wife back to the Americas, though it was my fortune he had his eye on. There is a side to him that he does not show often, a darker side.'

'Is Davis in England, then?' Gabriel tried to keep the fury from his tone.

'No.'

God, could Friar come back here, then, to Ravenshill Manor where it had all started? Was he after some sort of twisted vengeance with Adelaide as the bait? He held his wife closer and kissed her hair, but the darkening sky outside looked more threatening than it had done before and the lack of manpower at Ravenshill needed redressing.

He did not want to worry her with this, but he needed to be ready just in case. Standing, he stretched, trying to look nonchalant, but he should have realised that Adelaide's mind was turning as fast as his own.

'Would he come here, do you think? Would he be after you next because of Henrietta Clements?'

He smiled. God, this is what it was to be married. You forgot about yourself and thought of the other person. The stakes heightened and a new fear rose. If anything ever happened to Adelaide he would not survive. He knew that with a certainty that took the breath from him.

'We will be safe, sweetheart, I swear it.'

Gabriel sat at the window that night and looked across the land of Ravenshill before him. Bathed in the oncoming dusk he could see as far as the Barron Hills in one direction and the Scott River in the other. His land. Wesley land; land that had

been in the family for generations and generations, wrought in pain and protected in blood.

He felt safe here, he thought, because he knew
the lie of it, the hidden places and the valleys, the
streams and the meadows. Oh, granted, Henrietta had surprised him once in the chapel with
her madness and her delusions, but he was not
the same man that he had been then. Now he had
a purpose to live for, a reason for laying down
his life and protecting his family.

Adelaide. They might never have children, but
they would always have each other. His mind
wandered to clever dark-haired little girls with
smiles like their mother, but he shook the thought
away. Even given his love for his wife his libido
had not awakened. He swore beneath his breath,
but softly, for Adelaide was asleep behind him,
curled up in repose, and he did not wish to wake
her.

'Come on, you bastard,' he whispered and
his fingers curled around the barrel of his gun.
'Show yourself to me so that we can meet honestly and finish this.'

But nothing moved as the sky lightened and the dawn broke pink over the lush green landscape that was Ravenshill.

Chapter Seventeen

Daniel, Amethyst and baby Robert Wylde came to the Manor the next morning, stopping in on their way back to Montcliffe.

'Amethyst was fretting at Colton House and she wanted to be home, but we needed to tell you again, Adelaide, of how much we will always be in your debt. If there is ever any favour you wish from us…' Daniel Wylde stopped and shook his head. 'You would only need to ask and it shall be yours.'

'I would like your friendship,' she said and gave Amethyst a hug before taking the baby. He was small and beautiful with rosebud lips and a shock of dark hair. As unfocused blue eyes watched her own she smiled.

'He is Robert after my father,' Amethyst explained, her fingers stroking the downy head. When Adelaide looked up and saw her husband's eyes on her holding little Robert she also saw what no one else ever would.

Loss.

It was scrawled across the gold with a flaring damage. Fleeting and then hidden.

Did he think it mattered so very much to her? Did he imagine he was less of a man only because he could not father a child? Crossing the room, she laid the baby in his arms, liking the way his bigness cradled the fragility. Their circle of progeny might be broken, but others could be formed. Others like this child, one small hand winding its way around her husband's finger. Adelaide knew enough of life to understand the beauty of compromise.

'We shall always be here for you, little one,' she said softly. 'In good times and in bad.'

'Speaking of bad,' Daniel suddenly said, 'have you heard any more from the Service about Clements's death, Gabe?'

'I'm certain it was George Friar who killed him. Clement's cousin,' he clarified as Daniel looked puzzled. 'He was the one who stood to inherit any money. Friar told Adelaide he needed cash to inject into a Baltimore project, and with Henrietta dead there was only Randolph in the way.'

'But wouldn't others suspect him?'

'He set himself up an alibi with those who he'd been in cahoots with, men whose interest in politics did not quite reach to the shedding of blood for it. Friar undoubtedly was the one who did that and he chose his accomplices well.'

'Do you have proof?'

'Only the memory of Henrietta's last words. She told me about Friar before she threw herself into the flames, but I had not remembered it until yesterday.'

'A timely recollection, then. How dangerous is he, do you think?'

Gabriel ignored Daniel Wylde's question and posed one of his own. 'When you go back to Montcliffe, would you take my wife with you?'

'No.' Now Adelaide understood. 'I am going nowhere without you, Gabriel. We could both leave and then Lucien and Francis could help you, too.'

'Daniel will bring them back once he has seen you safe. Please, Adelaide. I can't think of you and Friar both and I am well able to look after myself here.'

Adelaide thought wildly. She could not ask Daniel to stay and assist Gabriel because he would want to be sure to shepherd his wife and baby to safety. And there would be a gap of hours that Gabriel would be all alone. She thought of the servants and knew they would be some help, but against a trained killer…?

'You would return to Ravenshill immediately?' This question she asked of Daniel.

'I would.'

'Then I will do as you ask, Gabriel.' She thought that her heart might just break there in that room with the jagged thought of leaving.

'Gabriel is the happiest I have ever seen him look,' Amethyst said as the carriage swept through the impressive lands of Ravenshill. 'Daniel says we should take to the game of

matchmaking with more alacrity as we are undoubtedly successful at it.'

'Where is your husband?' Laughing, Adelaide glanced outside to see if she could see Lord
Montcliffe on the horse he had mounted as they
left the house.

'He's scouting ahead probably. Just to be certain that it is safe and that all...'

Her words died on the sharp crack of a bullet
and then a second and third one. Any hope that
there was a hunter nearby died with the slowing
of the coach.

'My God, where is Daniel?' Amethyst
Wylde's panicked voice rose above the silence
and she tucked baby Robert into his tiny bed on
the floor and draped her skirts across him.

Protection.

Adelaide saw the look of it in her eyes even as
she swallowed back her own fright.

The carriage door opened a few seconds later
and George Friar stood there, a different man
from the way he had looked in London with a
bloodied bandage around his hand and in clothes
like those worn by the countryside peasants.

'Get out.' The gun he had was pointed straight at her and without thought she did as she was told, shutting the door behind her once she was through it and hoping it was only she that he was after.

Please, God, do not let the baby cry, she thought as she walked away with Friar towards his horse. *And please do not let Daniel ride over that ridge unarmed.*

So focused on trying to keep the Wyldes safe she had forgotten about her own well-being, and when Friar brought his hand up and slapped her with all the force he could muster, she fell at his feet. Would he kill her here before she had the chance to fight back? Dizziness made her feel sick.

'Get up.' His mouth was a hard slash as he hailed her to the horse. 'That is for slapping me at the ball and this is from Kenneth Davis.' This time he punched her in the stomach, a hard in-different fist that jammed the air from her wind-pipe and made her shake violently.

'Now keep quiet and you might live awhile

longer. It's your husband I want. He killed Henrietta and he needs to pay for it.'

'No. She…killed…herself…'

'Liar.'

He hit her again across the cheek before hauling her up on the horse. Adelaide knew it would only be a matter of hours before Gabriel came to find her and she prayed to God that the mad and dangerous George Friar had not killed the Earl of Montcliffe.

Red-hot anger filled Gabriel's head, anger that would not help anything.

The bastard had his wife. He had dragged her off out of the carriage and hit her. Hard. Amethyst had said so.

Daniel lay on the sofa with a bullet through his side, the kneeling apothecary trying to staunch the bleeding.

'Friar caught me…as I came through a glade… of trees. Knocked me clean off my horse and… out cold.'

'I found him after I had left the carriage. Our driver is dead and so is the other guard.' Tears trailed down Amethyst's cheeks and the grime of the day stained her clothes. Baby Robert had been taken upstairs, the housekeeper and two maids seeing to his every need.

'So he took the track through the river?' Gabriel asked again, already selecting guns and a knife from a cabinet in the corner.

It would be getting dark in a few hours. He had to find Adelaide before nightfall or else... Shades of what had happened to Henrietta Clements came to mind, but Gabriel pushed those away and barked out instructions to the few male servants he had kept on at Ravenshill after the fire.

'Lock the doors after I go and don't let anyone in, unless you can see it is me.' He shoved a gun into the hands of his elderly butler and gave another to the footman. 'Cover the house from each direction. If you see anything move, shoot first and ask questions later.'

Daniel had lost consciousness again now, his face pale and drawn.

'Can you fix him?' This was barked at Andrew McAuley, the local apothecary.

'Yes. It is a surface wound. The bullet passed through the muscle on both sides, which explains the bleeding, but it is already stopping. But he mustn't be moved for a good few hours until the blood sets.'

'Very well. Amethyst, find some blankets from upstairs and make him warm. Get the house-keeper to make you a hot drink as well. You are shaking.'

And with that he left, the house behind him and the greying dusk in front.

Friar had gone to the old homestead near the quarry, he thought, as he mounted his horse brought to him by one of the stablehands.

'I heard about your wife, sir, and I hope you find her soon. The building near the slopes of scree could be where he has taken her if the other lady was correct in her directions.'

'My thoughts exactly. I want you to go up to the house and get the butler to give you a gun. If I am not back by the morning, tell Lord Mont-cliffe to organise a search party and send for the constabulary. Go and find Alex Watkins, too, and make certain he is armed.'

'Very well, my lord,' the other answered, holding the reins as he mounted and then handing them to him. 'Good luck, sir.'

Then Ravenshill was behind him as was the growing, swirling wind. He'd have to be careful with that. If Friar's horse smelt his one...?

He left that thought alone and thundered onwards.

Adelaide was tied to a tree, the bindings at her neck cutting off breath so that she had to sit up and tip her head backwards slightly just to gain air.

Don't panic, she thought, as she watched George Friar. *Don't move, either.* He had split her lip as he had hauled her from the horse and she had a pounding headache from where he had knocked her unconscious with the back of his heavy knife in order to tie her down.

She was expendable now. Gabriel would come and it did not matter if she lived or died. Friar had made that point eminently plain.

'Do anything to annoy me and you are dead.'

The wind blew in steadily, a low and keening

cry as it hit the tall pines and whistled through them. The sound of her heart kept the rhythm of the wind, too, thump, thump, thump, in her ears heavy and hard.

She felt sick and began to shake. If she vomited, she would be dead, the oxygen she took nearly too minimal to allow life even as it was. She swallowed back the bile as well as she was able and thought of Gabriel.

If he came straight through the path, that would be the end of it, but this was his land and he would know the traps. She prayed Amethyst had thought to see which direction Friar had struck out in as spots of white began to dance in her eyes, heat rising like flame across her.

A slow death. Unnoticed. Degree by degree. She could not even whimper for fear that Friar would kill her. Heavy dread gathered across pure hate and the waste of everything spread over that.

To only just find happiness and then to lose it. She had finally understood what it was to be loved without reservation, without limits and now to have it snatched from her. No, she could not allow it.

Sitting up straighter, she tried to find the little air still left to her and clamped down upon her shaking.

'Please,' she whispered. 'Please.'

His wife was dead. He could see the whiteness across her face and the blood at her lip and eyes and head. The ropes had killed her, tightened by fear as a collar about her neck and from this distance he could see no movement and no breath. Her hands lay crooked at her sides like wooden marionettes in the Marais in Paris, abandoned after a puppet show.

Nothing mattered any more save to kill Friar. He came from the trees at the side with a guttural scream and fell upon the man before he had the chance to lift his gun.

One slice with his knife and another to the stomach; let him bleed out everywhere, his guts spilling on to the ground beneath him. A fitting end.

And then he was at the side of Adelaide, cutting the ties, loosening the ropes and laying her on the ground. Amazingly she took in breath, a huge gulp of air that changed her pallor from white to red in a matter of seconds and allowed her to lift one hand to his face, fingers shaking as she grasped his hair.

'You are…here. I prayed to God…that you would come, but…'

He simply lifted her, away from the cottage, away from the stinking, bleeding body of Friar, away from the ropes and the reminder of what had been. She was recovering quite rapidly, her arms gripping his and her voice stronger. He thanked the Lord for it.

'I love you, Gabriel. I knew you would come for me.'

When he sat her against the wall at the back of the house he began to laugh, the shock of escape perhaps, and the luck of it.

God. They were both alive and safe. She still lived and breathed and was. Alive.

The feeling of power hit him like a heavy blow right into the groin, taking the deadness and replacing it with pure and unadulterated lust. Vital. Quickened. Energetic. Any humour fled.

'I want you.' The words were out before he knew it.

'I want you, too, to forget,' she returned, reaching up and he lifted her skirts as she opened her legs. The blood beat through him out of control and frantic. If he wasn't within her he would die, it was that simple.

Not just want, either, but need, and not just need, but desperation.

When she bit into his shoulder to hurry him on, he moved her thighs over him and sank in, as far as he could go, claiming her as his own.

'Mine,' he cried as he felt the giving.

Her breath caught as the barrier of her virginity fell away and he stopped, dead still, giving her the time she might need to accommodate him, both their hearts beating in unison and desire. Her nails dug into his skin, keeping him close.

He rode her with the thought of possession, pressed in tight with the understanding that they could both be saved by it and survive with the oneness and the relief. Almost seven months of grief and loss flowed now into elation and when she shouted out and arched he went with her willingly, the spill of his seed deep in her womb as her muscles clenched and held him still.

Life and lifeless lay on each side of the same coin, happy and sad separated by a thread. This was the little death the French spoke of, the place where nothing else mattered save sensation, the suspension of energy whilst time stopped and each separate beat of two hearts lay perfectly merged, blended and united.

He turned her head and kissed her in the same hard way, deep and rough, and she kissed him back, without reserve or restraint, giving as good as taking.

This was not the time for a fragile tryst or a tentative trust. His body shook with the want of her and he felt himself harden again.

'I love you. I love you more than life itself and if I lost you…'

She placed a finger on his top lip.

'There are no ifs, Gabriel. I will never leave you.'

She smiled as she drew him back in, guiding

him to the slickness of her centre. This time his ardour was quieter and more tempered, fierceness buffered and held in check. The wrath was gone, but the wonderment still lived on, her warmth and her tightness. The bruising around her neck was already turning black and the cut on her head had begun to bleed. But he could not stop and tend to her just yet, the shake of fear still in him, the fright of loss unquenched. He felt the crescendo before it even came, cutting into him like a hot knife across butter, the relief of it making him shout her name again and again in pure and honest gratitude. The noise of the pines above snatched the sound away.

Afterwards Gabriel took her in his lap and wrapped her with his cloak so that they were enfolded in the darkness and the quiet. The moon had risen, the light of it spilling through the trees and across them both.

Unreal and shadowed.

'You are no longer impotent?' There was humour in her whisper and he drew his hands through his hair.

'Rage has cured me, I think, and fear. When I

first saw you I thought you were dead and then I was in you, scrambling for life and love and for ever.'

In the moonlight he saw her smile. 'I think all those rumours about your prowess might very well be true. But from now your expertise is only for my benefit.'

When he laughed the sound travelled through the glade and then echoed back, the small joy bouncing and reverberating against the trees. Like music.

It was his life now. Complete. Adelaide had brought him that. Acceptance. Resurrection. Absolution.

He looked upwards into the heavens and thanked God for bringing her to him, through the darkness of his life and into the light.

They arrived back at Ravenshill at midnight to find Daniel Wylde had been put to bed and that the bleeding on his side had stopped hours ago. Amethyst came to meet them at the doorway and when she saw Adelaide she took her into her arms.

'Thank God you are safe. Thank God we are all safe. Your housekeeper made us take your room, Gabriel, but I can always move Daniel...'

'No. We will sleep in the cottage at the back.'

'You are sure? Did you see your neighbour— Alexander Watkins, I think he said was his name? He came looking for you.'

'Yes. He helped me clean up...things and then went to get the constabulary. That's why we have been so long.'

A cry from Robert had Amethyst turning.

'We shall have to talk in the morning.' She smiled at both of them and then went back into the annex, leaving Gabriel and Adelaide to gather a few things and then make their way outside.

The world seemed softer tonight, more gentle after the terrible day, and Gabriel was glad for it.

Once in the cottage he made certain the lock on the door was secure and then lit a few of the candles he had brought over from the annex. Taking off their clothes, they jumped beneath the heavy eiderdown and settled against the cushioned bedhead.

'I think George Friar actually loved Henrietta

Clements, despite all that she said of him, Gabriel. He repeated over and over that he wanted you to feel the anguish he knew in losing her. He still thought it was you who had killed her despite everything that was decided by the courts. He said you had paid them off.'

'But she threw herself into the fire after lighting it.'

'I told him that, too, but...' She stopped.

'He did not believe it.'

'Friar said her husband had never loved her properly, either. But he didn't kill him. Friar said John Goode had done that himself because of money Randolph Clements had taken, money that was supposed to go to the coffers of France.'

'A hive of iniquity, then, with no one trusting the other?'

'These were the sort of people you stopped, weren't they? The ones who would cause havoc on society out of madness and hate if they were just left? It must have been horrible to be amongst them and to pretend.'

He frowned. 'I did not always have to pretend, Adelaide.'

'I know. Tonight… I could tell you had…done that before.'

'Espionage has the same rules of war. Kill or be killed.' He took her hand, his fingers threading though her own, holding on. 'It was not always easy and it wasn't always right.'

'Can you stop, then…working for the Service, I mean?'

'I almost have. I will send the names to Alan Wolfe tomorrow and they will be rounded up and questioned. There is enough proof of foul play to put them in jail, I think, and that will be the end of it.'

'And then we can live here at Ravenshill and farm and rebuild and…' She stopped and blushed as his eyes looked closely at her face.

'Is this sore?' Her lip was swollen and there was another bruise on her cheek. In the candlelight he could see so much more than he had been able to outside the cottage and his anger against George Friar returned.

'I hope I did not hurt you when…'

She finished the sentence. 'When you made

love to me as if I was the only woman left in the world.'

'The only one I love, at least. As you know, I thought you were dead when I saw you in the clearing tied to the tree and I wondered if I could ever live again. It is a rare thing to have your life held in the hand of another and not want it different, I think. To belong to someone, I mean, for ever, and be the happier for it.'

'My old aunts used to say that independence was the key to a good life and for a long time I believed them. Until you. Until you smiled at me and asked me questions at the Bradford ball with your golden eyes and your quick-witted words. You smelt like woodsmoke and leather and I thought I had never had another conversation like it.'

'I should have touched you then and there and felt the magic. I should have taken the chance and grabbed your hand and kissed you and carted you off to Gretna Green. Instead, I watched you dance a waltz with the Earl of Berrick and he held you much too close.'

'Close like this?'

She wrapped her arms about his neck and pulled him down into the nest of duck feathers.

This time she wanted to be the one in control, the one to set the pace and the tone. Her mouth closed over his nipple and she took him hard, like he had taken her against the wall of the abandoned building, unyielding and fierce in the dark.

Biting the skin across the plane of his stomach, she went lower and saw the damage that he had not wanted her to see, the swathe of burned skin across his upper-right thigh and groin.

She knew he waited to see just what she might say for his breath stopped and his fingers clenched the softness of the cotton sheets beneath, the wedding ring he wore catching the candlelight.

With care she traced the ruin with her tongue, along this ridge of damage and then down to the next. Always coming closer to the hard shaft that lay amidst a bush of light-brown hair, only a small burn marking the smoothness.

And then he was inside her, the taste of him

salty and masculine, sweet and known. So easy to make him hers, she thought, the rise of him sure and quick now. The power of what he allowed her boiled in her blood, too, a shared joy, a further intimacy that held no words, but only feeling. Then the thickening, as the tempo changed to a reaching, surging ache of trust.

Gabriel. Her angel delivered from Heaven.

'I love you.' Whispered on the edge of tears, her voice quiet with feeling. He had killed a man to protect her and then banished her demons with his own body. Only strength in it and an undeniable honesty, because in the gift he gave her she had lost all fear.

He lifted her upwards and took her mouth into his own, other flavours, further discoveries. Abandoned and open she accepted him in and she writhed with the beauty of it and the truth. She was no longer only herself. He was of her, inside, curling around constant loneliness and ancient shame. There were no rules here, no inhibitions, no places the ache of knowledge could not touch as love accompanied the sensual.

'I love you, Gabriel. Till for ever.'

'Make a child with me, then. Here and now. Let this be the moment of his conception, in this bed with the moon outside and Ravenshill safe. But this time together and in gentleness. This time only with love.'

'Yes.' She felt tears fill her eyes, not of sadness but of joy. She felt his hardness and her own answering push. She felt the starch of cotton beneath them and the cool of the night on their skin. She smelt the wax of a candle and heard the call of an owl, far away in the lines of trees that ran behind the high ground where a house could be rebuilt.

Home. Here. With Gabriel.

And then as he came within her and his fingers found that place that only he could know, she closed her eyes and simply was.

* * * * *

Sophia James's
THE PENNILESS LORDS
continues with Lucien's story.
Coming soon.